THE
CAINE PRIZE
FOR AFRICAN
WRITING 2019
SHORTLIST

Individual contributions © The Authors, 2018.

Cover illustration: Flores/Unsplash

Design by New Internationalist.

Printed by TJ International Ltd, Cornwall, UK, who hold environmental accreditation ISO 14001

British Library Cataloguing-in-Publication Data.
A catalogue record for this book is available from the British Library.

ISBN 978-1-78026-520-9

Contents

Foreword

The 20th shortlist for the Caine Prize for African Writing was selected from 131 entries from 21 African countries by an eminent panel of judges chaired by Dr Peter Kimani, author of the critically acclaimed *Dance of the Jakaranda*. Joining Dr Kimani on the panel of judges are: Nigerian playwright and novelist, Sefi Atta; author and award-winning journalist, Margie Orford; Professor Scott Taylor from Georgetown University; and writer and essayist, Olufemi Terry, winner of the 2010 Caine Prize for African Writing. They have the joyful task of selecting a winner from a shortlist that offers a tantalizing hint of the sheer diversity of African writing today.

Commenting on the shortlist, Dr Kimani said: 'Without exception, past Caine Prize winners have been revolutionary and evolutionary – breaking fresh ground, while pushing the African story from the margins to the mainstream of world literature. The five writers on this year's shortlist carry on with that tradition, not just in their inventiveness in imagining the world, but also in tackling the ordinary in an extraordinary manner, taking in a wide range of issues: gender and generation; home and exile; sexuality and religion; love and hate; happiness and heartbreak.'

Recent years have seen significant changes at the Caine Prize. There have been two successive African chairs in the persons respectively of Dr Delia Jarrett-Macauley and Ellah Wakatama Allfrey OBE. The new Caine Prize administrator is Dele Meiji Fatunla. Despite these changes, the central purpose of the Prize – to celebrate the best of Africa's storytelling tradition – remains the same, and we hope you find that this year's shortlist continues to reflect the boldness, diversity and sheer creativity of African writers today. It is pleasing that the stories come both from countries that have frequently appeared on our shortlists, Kenya and Nigeria, as well as from two less often represented, Cameroon and Ethiopia, reflecting the expanding opportunities to African writers that the Prize has done much to bring about. We hope these stories delight, challenge and expand your understanding of the African experience and storytelling.

The winner of the 20th Caine Prize for African Writing will be announced and awarded at the School of Oriental and African Studies for the third time, through the generous support of SOAS Director, Baroness Amos, and our sponsors. The principal sponsors of the 2019 Prize are the Oppenheimer Memorial Trust, the Booker Prize Foundation, Miles Morland, the Wyfold Trust, the Sigrid Rausing Trust, John Niepold, Adam Freudenheim, Arindam Bhattacharjee, Antoine Van Aegtmael and Phillip Ihenacho. We have received generous support in kind from the Royal Overseas League, the British Council, the Royal African Society, SOAS (Centre of African Studies) and Georgetown University. We are grateful for this generous support without which the Caine Prize would not be Africa's leading literary award.

Ellah Wakatama Allfrey OBE
Chair of Trustees, the Caine Prize for African Writing

Dele Meiji Fatunla,
Administrator of the Caine Prize for African Writing

The 2019 panel of judges

Peter Kimani began his career as a journalist and is the author of several works of poetry and prose, including 2017's internationally acclaimed *Dance of the Jakaranda*, a *New York Times* Notable Book of the Year. A former senior editor at *The Standard*, Kimani has also appeared in *The Guardian*, the *New African*, Sky News and the *Daily Nation*. He was awarded a doctorate in Creative Writing and Literature from the University of Houston in 2014, and currently teaches at the Aga Khan University's Graduate School of Media and Communications in Nairobi.

Sefi Atta was born in Lagos, Nigeria, in 1964. She is the author of *Everything Good Will Come* (2005), *News from Home* (2010), *Swallow* (2010), *A Bit of Difference* (2013), *Drama Queen* (2018), *The Bead Collector* (2019) and the forthcoming *Sefi Atta: Selected Plays* (2019). She was a juror for the 2010 Neustadt International Prize for Literature, and has received several literary awards for her works, including the 2006 Wole Soyinka Prize for Literature in Africa and the 2009 Noma Award for Publishing in Africa. Her radio plays have been broadcast by the BBC and her stage plays have been performed and published internationally.

Margie Orford is an internationally acclaimed writer. Her Clare Hart novels – a literary crime-fiction series that explores violence and its effects in South Africa – are published in the US and the UK and have been widely translated into more than ten languages. They include *Like Clockwork* (2006), *Blood Rose* (2006),

Gallows Hill (2009), *Daddy's Girl* (2011), and *Water Music* (2013). They have led to her being described by *The Weekender* as the 'queen of South African crime-thriller writers.' She is also an award-winning journalist who writes for papers in the United Kingdom and South Africa. Apart from her fiction, she writes regularly about crime, gender violence, politics and freedom of expression.

Scott Taylor is professor and director of the African Studies Program in the Edmund A Walsh School of Foreign Service at Georgetown University. Originally from New York, he has studied, worked and travelled widely in Africa for three decades, and has resided in both Zambia and Zimbabwe. He received his MA and PhD in political science from Emory University, and an AB in Government from Dartmouth College. As an academic, his research and teaching interests lie in the areas of African politics and political economy, with a particular emphasis on governance and political and economic reform. His articles have appeared in numerous political science and area studies journals, and he is the author of four books: *Politics in Southern Africa: Transition and Transformation*; *Culture and Customs of Zambia*; *Business and the State in Southern Africa: The Politics of Economic Reform*; and *Globalization and the Cultures of Business in Africa: From Patrimonialism to Profit.*

Olufemi Terry, a freelance writer, essayist and journalist based in Washington, DC, is the Sierra Leone-born winner of the 2010 Caine Prize for African Writing. His fiction has been translated into French and German, and was published most recently in the *One World Two* global anthology of short stories.

The Caine Prize 2019
Shortlisted Stories

Skinned

Lesley Nnneka Arimah

The unclothed woman had a neatly trimmed bush, waxed to resemble a setting sun. The clothed women sneered as she laid out makeup and lotion samples, touting their benefits. 'Soft, smooth skin, as you can see,' she said, winking – trying, and failing, to make a joke of her nakedness. Chidinma smiled in encouragement, nodding and examining everything Ejem pulled out of the box. Having invited Ejem to present her wares, she would be getting a free product out of this even if none of her guests made a purchase.

Ejem finished her sales pitch with a line about how a woman's skin is her most important feature and she has to take care of it like a treasured accessory. The covered women tittered and smoothed their tastefully patterned wife-cloth over their limbs. They wore them simply, draped and belted into long, graceful dresses, allowing the fabric to speak for itself. They eyed Ejem's nakedness with gleeful pity.

'I just couldn't be uncovered at your age. That's a

thing for the younger set, don't you think?'

'I have a friend who's looking for a wife; maybe I can introduce you. He's not picky.'

Ejem rolled her eyes, less out of annoyance than to keep tears at bay. Was this going to happen every time? She looked to Chidinma for help.

'Well, I for one am here for lotions, not to discuss covered versus uncovered, so I'd like this one.' Chidinma held up the most expensive cream. Ejem made a show of ringing it up and the other women were embarrassed into making purchases of their own. They stopped speaking to Ejem directly and began to treat her as if she were a woman of the osu caste. They addressed product questions to the air or to Chidinma, and listened but did not acknowledge Ejem when she replied. Ejem might have protested, as would have Chidinma, but they needed the sales party to end before Chidinma's husband returned. It was the only stipulation Chidinma had made when she'd agreed to host. It was, in fact, the only stipulation of their friendship. Don't advertise your availability to my husband. Chidinma always tried to make a joking compliment of it – 'You haven't had any kids yet, so your body is still amazing' – but there was always something strained there, growing more strained over the years as Ejem remained unclaimed.

The woman who had first addressed Chidinma instead of Ejem, whom Ejem had begun to think of as the ringleader, noticed them glancing at the clock, gave a sly smile, and requested that each and every product be explained to her. Ejem tried, she really did, whipping through the product texts with speed, but the clock sped just as quickly and eventually Chidinma stopped helping her, subdued by inevitable embarrassment. Before long, Chidinma's husband returned from work.

Chance was all right, as husbands went. He oversaw the management of a few branches of a popular bank, a job that allowed them to live comfortably in their large house with an osu woman to spare Chidinma serious housework. He could even be considered somewhat progressive; after all, he had permitted his wife's continued association with her unclothed friend, and he wasn't the sort to harass an osu woman in his employ. True, he insisted on a formal greeting, but after Chidinma had bowed to him she raised herself to her tiptoes for a kiss and Chance indulged her, fisting his hands in the wife-cloth at the small of her back.

But he was still a man, and when he turned to greet the women his eyes caught on Ejem and stayed there, taking in the brown discs of her areolae, the cropped design of hair between her legs, whatever parts of her went unhidden in her seated position. No one said anything, the utter impropriety of an unclaimed woman being in the house of a married man almost too delicious a social faux pas to interrupt. But, as Chidinma grew visibly distressed, the ringleader called the room to order and the women rose to leave, bowing their heads to Chance, giving Chidinma's hands encouraging little squeezes. No doubt the tale would make the rounds – 'the way he stared at her' – and Chidinma wouldn't be able to escape it for a while. The women walked by Ejem without a word, the message clear: Ejem was beneath them.

Chidinma tried to distract her husband by asking about his day. Chance continued to stare at Ejem while he answered. Ejem wanted to move faster, to get out as quick as she could, but she was conscious of every sway of her breasts, every brush of her thighs as she hurried. Chance spoke to Ejem only as she was leaving, a goodbye she returned with a small curtsy. Chidinma walked her to the door.

'Ejem, we should take a break from each other, I think,' she said with a pained air of finality, signaling that this break wasn't likely to be a temporary one.

'Why?'

'You know why.'

'You're going to have to say it, Chidinma.'

'Fine. This whole thing, this friendship, was fine when we were both uncovered girls doing whatever, but covered women can't have uncovered friends. I thought it was nonsense at first, but it's true. I'm sorry.'

'You've been covered for thirteen years and this has never been a problem.'

'And I thought by this time you'd be covered, too. You came so close with that one fellow, but you've never really tried. It's unseemly.'

'He's only seen me this once since you made it clear–'

'Once was enough. Get covered. Get claimed. Take yourself off the market. Until then, I'm sorry, but no.'

Chidinma went back inside the house before Ejem could respond. And what could she say anyway? I'm not sure I ever want to be claimed? Chidinma would think her mad.

Ejem positioned her box to better cover her breasts and walked to the bus stop. Chidinma hadn't offered her a ride home, even though she knew how much Ejem hated public transportation – the staring as she lay the absorbent little towel square on her seat, the paranoia of imagining every other second what to do if her menstrual cup leaked.

At the stop, a group of young men waited. They stopped talking when they saw Ejem, then resumed, their conversation now centred on her.

'How old you think she is?'

'Dude, old.'

'I don't know, man. Let's see her breasts. She should put that box down.'

They waited and Ejem ignored them, keeping as much of herself as possible shielded with the box and the cosmetic company's branded tote.

'That's why she's unclaimed. Rudeness. Who's gonna want to claim that?'

They continued in that vein until the bus arrived.

Even though the men were to board first, they motioned her ahead, a politeness that masked their desire for a better view. She scanned the passengers for other uncovered women – solidarity and all that – and was relieved to spot one. The relief quickly evaporated. The woman was beautiful, which would have stung on its own, but she was young, too, smooth-skinned and firm. Ejem stopped existing for the group of young men. They swarmed the woman, commenting loudly on the indentation of her waist, the solid curve of her arm. The young woman took it all in stride, scrolling a finger down the pages of her book.

Ejem felt at once grateful and slighted, remembering how it had been in her youth, before her waist had thickened and her ass drooped. She'd never been the sort to wear nakedness boldly, but she'd at least felt that she was pleasant to look at.

The bus took on more passengers and was three-quarters full when an osu woman boarded. Ejem caught herself doing a double take before averting her gaze. It wasn't against the law; it just wasn't done, since the osu had their own transport, and the other passengers looked away as well. Embarrassed. Annoyed. Even the bus driver kept his eyes forward as the woman counted out her fare. And when she finally appeared in the center aisle, no one made the polite shift all passengers on public transportation know, that nonverbal invitation to take a neighboring seat. So even though there were several spots available, the osu woman remained standing. Better that than climb her naked body over another to sit down. It was the type of subtle social correction, Ejem thought, that would cause a person to behave better in the future.

But as the ride progressed, the osu woman squeezing to let by passengers who didn't even acknowledge her, Ejem softened. She was so close to becoming an unseen woman herself, unanchored from the life and the people she knew, rendered invisible. It was only by the grace of birth that she wasn't osu, her mother had said to her the very last time they spoke. 'At least you have a choice, Ejem. So choose wisely.' She hadn't, had walked away from a man and his proposal and the protection it offered. Her parents had cut her off then, furious and confounded that she'd bucked tradition. She couldn't explain, not even to herself, why she'd looked at the cloth he proffered and seen a weight that would smother her.

At her stop, Ejem disembarked, box held to her chest. With the exception of a few cursory glances, no one paid attention to her. It was one of the reasons she liked the city, everybody's inclination to mind their own business. She picked up the pace when she spotted the burgundy awning of her apartment building. In the elevator, an older male tenant examined her out of the corner of his eye. Ejem backed up until he would have had to turn around to continue looking. One could never tell if a man was linked or not, and she hated being inspected by men who'd already claimed wives.

In her apartment she took a long, deep breath, the type she didn't dare take in public lest she draw unwanted attention. Only then did she allow herself to contemplate the loss of Chidinma's friendship, and weep.

When they were girls, still under their fathers' covering, she and Chidinma had become fast friends. They were both new to their school and their covers were so similar in pattern they were almost interchangeable. Ejem remembered their girlhood fondly, the protection of their fathers' cloth, the seemingly absolute security of it. She had cried when, at fifteen, her mother had come into her bedroom and, stroking her hair, told Ejem that it was time to remove her cloth. The only people who could get away with keeping their daughters covered for long were the wealthy, who often managed it until the girls could secure wife-cloth. But Ejem's father had grown up a poor man in a village where girls were disrobed as early as possible, some even at age ten, and it was beyond time as far as he was concerned. He knew what happened to the families of girls who stayed covered beyond their station, with the exception of girls bearing such deformities that they were permitted 'community cloth' made from donated scraps. But if a girl like Ejem continued to be clothed, the town council would levy a tax that would double again and again until her father could not pay it. Then his girl would be disrobed in public, and her family shamed. No, he couldn't bear the humiliation. Things would happen on his terms.

The day Ejem was disrobed was also the day her father stopped interacting with her, avoiding the impropriety of a grown man talking to a naked girl. Ejem hadn't wanted to go to school or market or anywhere out of the house where people could see her. Chidinma, still under her father-cloth, told her (horrified, well-off) parents that she, too, felt ready to disrobe so that she and Ejem could face the world together, two naked foundlings.

Chidinma's parents had tried to spin it as piousness, a daughter disrobed earlier than she had to be because she was so dedicated to tradition. But it'd had the stink of fanaticism and they'd lost many friends, something for which, Chidinma confided, her parents had never forgiven her.

A part of Ejem had always believed they'd be claimed at the same time, but then Chidinma had secured a wife-cloth at twenty, with Ejem as her chief maid. And then Chidinma gave birth to a boy, then two girls, who would remain covered their entire lives if Chidinma had anything to say about it. And through it all, Ejem remained uncovered, unclaimed, drifting until the likelihood passed her by.

She downed a mug of wine in one huge gulp, then another, before sifting through yesterday's mail. She opened the envelope she'd been avoiding: the notice of her upcoming lease renewal, complete with a bump in monthly rent. With the money she'd earned today, she had enough to cover the next two months. But the raised rent put everything in jeopardy, and Chidinma's abandonment meant Ejem could no longer sell to her wealthy set. If she couldn't secure income some other way, a move to a smaller town would soon be a necessity.

When she'd first leased the apartment, Ejem had been working at the corporate headquarters of an architecture firm. Though her nakedness drew some attention, there were other unclaimed women, and Ejem, being very good at what she did, advanced. Just shy of a decade later, she was over thirty, the only woman in upper management, and still uncovered.

Three months ago, Ejem had been delivering a presentation to a prospective client. As usual, she was the only woman in the room. The client paid no attention to her PowerPoint, focusing instead on what he considered to be the impropriety of an unclaimed woman distracting from business matters. Ejem was used to this and tried to steer the conversation back to the budget. When the man ignored her, none of her co-workers bothered to censure him, choosing instead to snicker into their paperwork. She walked out of the room.

Ejem had never gone to Human Resources before; she'd always sucked it up. The HR manager, a covered woman who was well into her fifties, listened to her with a bored expression, then, with a pointed look at Ejem's exposed breasts, said: 'You can't seriously expect a group of men to pay attention to pie charts or whatever when there is an available woman in the room. Maybe if you were covered this wouldn't happen. Until you are, we can no longer put you in front of clients.'

Ejem walked out of the building and never returned. She locked herself away at home until Chidinma came knocking with a bottle of vodka, her youngest girl on her hip, and a flyer for home-based work selling makeup.

Now that lifeline was gone, and it would be only a matter of time until Ejem exhausted her savings. She switched on the TV, and flipped channels until she reached an uncovered young woman relating the news. The woman reported on a building fire in Onitsha and Ejem prepared dinner with the broadcast playing in the background, chopping vegetables for stir-fry until she registered the phrase 'unclaimed women' repeated several times. She turned up the volume.

The newscaster had been joined by an older man with a paternal air, who gave more details.

'The building was rumored to be a haven of sorts for unclaimed women, who lived there, evading their responsibilities as cloth makers. Authorities halted firefighters from putting out the blaze, hoping to encourage these lost women to return to proper life. At least three bodies were discovered in the ashes. Their identities have yet to be confirmed.'

That was the other reason Ejem wanted to remain in the metro area. Small towns were less tolerant of unclaimed women, some going so far as to outlaw their presence unless they were menials of the osu caste. They had a certain freedom, Ejem thought – these osu women who performed domestic tasks, the osu men who labored in the mines or constructed the buildings she'd once designed – though her envy was checked by the knowledge that it was a freedom born of irrelevance. The only place for unclaimed women, however, as far as most were concerned, was the giant factories, where they would weave cloth for women more fortunate than they.

The town's mayor appeared at a press conference.

'This is a decent town with decent people. If folks want to walk around uncovered and unclaimed, they need to go somewhere else. I'm sorry about the property loss and the folks who couldn't get out, but this is a family town. We have one of the world's finest factories bordering us. They could have gone there.' The screen flipped back to the newsman, who nodded sagely, his expression somehow affirming the enforcement of moral values even as it deplored the loss of life.

Ejem battled a bubble of panic. How long before her finances forced her out into the hinterlands, where she would have to join the cloth makers? She needed a job and she needed it fast.

What sorts of jobs could one do naked? Ejem was too old for anything entry-level, where she'd be surrounded day after day by twentysomethings who would be claimed quickly. Instead, she looked for jobs where her nudity would be less of an issue. She lasted at a nursing home for five weeks, until a visiting relative objected to her presence. At the coffee shop she made it two and a half hours until she had to hide in the back to avoid a former co-worker. She quit the next day. Everywhere she went heightened how sheltered she'd been at her corporate job. The farther from the center of town she searched, the more people stared at her openly, asking outright why she wasn't covered when they saw that she didn't bear the mark of an osu woman. Every once in a while Ejem encountered osu women forced outside by errands, branded by shaved heads with scarification scored above one ear. Other pedestrians avoided them as though they were poles or mailboxes or other such sidewalk paraphernalia. But Ejem saw them.

As her search became more desperate, every slight took a knife's edge, so that Ejem found herself bothered even by the young girls still covered in their father-cloth who snickered at her, unaware or not caring that they, too, would soon be stripped of protection. The worst were the pitying Oh, honey looks, the whispered assurances from older covered women that someone would eventually claim her.

After a while she found work giving massages at a spa. She enjoyed being where everyone was disrobed; the artificial equality was a balm. Her second week on the job, a woman walked in covered with one of the finest wife-cloths Ejem had ever seen. She ordered the deluxe package, consisting of every single service the spa offered.

'And may I have your husband's account number?'

'My account number,' the woman emphasized, sliding her card across the counter.

The desk girl glared at the card, glared at the woman, then left to get the manager. Everyone in the waiting room stared.

The manager, a woman close to Ejem's age, sailed in, her haughty manner turning deferential and apologetic as soon as she caught sight of the client. 'I'm so sorry. The girl is new, still in father-cloth. Please excuse her.' The finely clothed one remained silent. 'We will, of course, offer you a significant discount on your services today. Maria is ready to start on your massage right away.'

'No,' the woman said firmly. 'I want her to do it.' Ejem, who'd been pretending to straighten products on the shelves, turned to see the woman pointing at her.

Soon she was in one of the treatment rooms, helping the woman to disrobe, feeling the texture of the cloth, wanting to rub it against her cheek. She left to hang it and encountered the manager, who dragged her down the hall and spoke in a harsh whisper.

'Do you know who that is? That is Odinaka, the Odinaka. If she leaves here less than pleased, you will be fired. I hope I'm clear.'

Ejem nodded, returning to the massage room in a nervous daze. Odinaka was one of a handful of independently wealthy women who flouted convention without consequences. She was unclaimed, but covered herself anyway, and not in modest cloth, either, but in fine, bold fabric that invited attention and scrutiny. She owned almost half the cloth factories across the globe. This unthinkable rebellion drew criticism, but her wealth ensured that it remained just that: words but no action.

Odinaka sat on the massage table, swinging her legs. At Ejem's direction, she lay on her stomach while Ejem warmed oil between her hands. She coated Odinaka's ankles before sliding up to her calves, warming the tissue with her palms. She asked a few casual questions, trying to gauge whether she was a talker or preferred her massages silent. She needn't have worried. Not only did Odinaka give verbose replies, she had questions for Ejem herself. Before long, she had pried from Ejem the story of how she'd come to be here, easing muscle tensions instead of pursuing a promising career as an architect.

'It doesn't seem fair, does it, that you have to remain uncovered?'

Ejem continued with the massage, unsure how to reply to such seditious sentiments.

'You know, you and I are very similar,' Odinaka continued.

Ejem studied the woman's firm body, toned and slim from years of exercise. She considered the other ways in which they were different, not least that Odinaka had never had to worry about a bill in her life. She laughed.

'You are very kind, but we're nothing alike, though we may be of the same age,' she responded, as lightly as she could, tilting the ending into a question. Odinaka ignored it, turning over to face her.

'I mean it; we are both ambitious women trying to make our way unclaimed in male-dominated fields.'

Except, Ejem didn't say, you are completely free in a way I am not, as covered as you wish to be.

'Covering myself would be illegal–' she started.

'Illegal-smeagle. When you have as much money as I do, you exist above every law. Now, wouldn't you like to be covered too?'

Odinaka was her savior. She whisked Ejem away from her old apartment, helping her pay the fee to break her lease, and moved her into a building she owned in one of the city's nicest neighborhoods. Ejem's quarters, a two-bedroom apartment complete with a generously sized kitchen, had the freshness of a deep clean, like it had been long vacant, or had gone through a recent purge, stripped of the scent and personality of its previous occupant. The unit had a direct intercom to the osu women who took care of the place. Ejem was to make cleaning requests as needed, or requests for groceries that later appeared in her fridge. When Ejem mentioned the distance from the apartment to her job, Odinaka revealed that she didn't have to work if she didn't want to, and it was an easy choice not to return to the spa. The free time enabled her to better get to know the other women in the building.

There was Delilah, who seemed like a miniature Odinaka in dress and mannerisms, but in possession of only half as much confidence. Doreen, a woman close to forty, became Ejem's favorite. She owned a bookstore – one that did well as far as bookstores went – and she had the air of someone who knew exactly who she was and liked it. She eschewed the option to self-clothe.

'Let them stare,' Doreen would declare after a few glasses of wine. 'This body is a work of art.' She would lift her breasts with her hands, sending Ejem and the other women into tipsy giggles.

The remaining women – Morayo, Mukaso and Maryam – were polite but distant, performing enough social niceties to sidestep any allegations of rudeness, but only just. Ejem and Doreen called them the three Ms or, after a few drinks, 'Mmm, no,' for their recalcitrance. They sometimes joined in Odinaka's near-nightly cocktail hour, but within a few weeks the cadre solidified into Odinaka, Delilah, Doreen and Ejem.

With this group of women, there were no snide remarks about Ejem's nakedness, no disingenuous offers to introduce her to a man – any man – who could maybe look past her flaws. Odinaka talked about her vast business, Doreen about her small one, and they teased each other with terrible advice neither would ever take. Ejem talked some about the career she'd left behind, but didn't have much to add. And for the first time, her shyness was just shyness, not evidence of why she remained unclaimed, nor an invitation to be battered with advice on how she could improve herself.

Besides, Odinaka talked enough for everyone, interrupting often and dominating every topic. Ejem didn't mind, because of all of them, Odinaka had had the most interesting life, one of unrelenting luxury since birth. She'd inherited the weaving company from her father when he retired, almost a decade ago, which had caused an uproar. But if one of the wealthiest dynasties wanted a woman at the helm, it was a luxury they could purchase. And if that woman indulged in covering herself and collecting and caring for other unclaimed women, who had the power to stop her?

'I imagine creating a world,' Odinaka often said, 'where disrobing is something a woman does only by choice.'

On Ejem's first night in the building, Odinaka had brought a length of cloth to her, a gift, she said, that Ejem could wear whenever she wanted. Ejem had stared at the fabric for hours. Even in the confines of the building, in her own unit, she didn't have the courage to put it on. At Odinaka's cocktail hour, Doreen would sit next to her and declare, 'It's us against these bashful fuckers, Ejem,' setting off an evening of gentle ribbing at everyone's expense.

'You really go to your store like that?' Ejem asked Doreen one afternoon. 'Why don't you cover yourself? No one will say anything if they know you're one of Odinaka's women, right?' She was trying to convince herself that she, too, could don the cloth and go out in public without fear.

Doreen stopped perusing invoices to give Ejem all her attention. 'Look, we have to live with this. I was disrobed at age ten. Do you know what it feels like to be exposed so young? I hid for almost a decade before I found myself, my pride. No one will ever again make me feel uncomfortable in my own skin. I plan to remain unclaimed and uncovered for as long as I live, and no one can say a damn thing about it. Odinaka rebels in her own way, and I in mine. I don't yearn for the safety of cloth. If the law requires me to be naked, I will be naked. And I will be goddamned if they make me feel uncomfortable for their law.'

The weeks of welcome, of feeling free to be her own person, took hold and, one night, when Ejem joined the other women in Odinaka's apartment, she did so covered, the cloth draped over her in a girl's ties, the only way she knew how. Doreen was the first one to congratulate her, and when she hugged Ejem, she whispered, 'Rebel in your own way', but her smile was a little sad.

Odinaka crowed in delight: 'Another one! We should have a party.'

She mobilized quickly, dispensing orders to her osu women via intercom. Ejem had yet to see any of the osu at work, but whenever she returned to her quarters from Odinaka's or Doreen's, her bed was made, the bathroom mirror cleared of flecks, the scabs of toothpaste scrubbed from the sink, and the rooms themselves held an indefinable feeling of having only just been vacated.

In less than the hour it took Ejem and the other residents to get themselves ready for the party, Odinaka's quarters had become packed. Men and women, all clothed except Doreen, mingled and chatted. Doreen held court on the settee, sipping wine and bestowing coy smiles.

Ejem tried to join in, but even with the self-cloth, she couldn't help feeling like the uncovered woman she'd been her entire adult life. Odinaka tried to draw Ejem into her circle of conversation, but after Ejem managed only a few stilted rejoinders, she edged away, sparing herself further embarrassment. Ejem ended up in a corner watching the festivities.

She was not aware that she herself was being watched until a man she'd seen bowing theatrically to Odinaka leaned against the wall next to her.

'So, you're the newest one, huh?'

'I suppose I am.'

'You seem reasonable enough. Why are you unclaimed?'

Ejem tensed, wary.

'What's that supposed to mean, "reasonable"?'

He ignored the question.

'Do you know I have been trying to claim that woman ever since she was a girl?' He nodded toward Odinaka. 'Our union would have been legendary. The greatest cloth weaver with the greatest cotton grower. What do you think?'

Ejem shrugged. It was really none of her business.

'Instead she's busy collecting debris.'

Stunned by his rudeness, Ejem turned away, but he only laughed and called to someone across the room. Suddenly every laugh seemed directed at her, every smile a smirk at her expense. She felt herself regressing into the girl who'd needed Chidinma's tight grip in hers before she could walk with her head high. She ducked out, intending to return to her quarters.

She ran into Delilah, who held a carved box under her arm, a prized family heirloom Ejem recognized from their many gatherings. It was one of the few objects Odinaka envied, as she could not secure one herself, unable to determine the origin of the antique. She was forever demanding that Delilah bring it out to be admired, though Delilah refused to let Odinaka have it examined or appraised, perfectly content to let her treasure remain a mystery.

Ejem didn't particularly like Delilah. She might have been a mini Odinaka but, unlike Odinaka,

Delilah was pretentious and wore her fine breeding on her sleeve. Ejem's distress was visible enough that Delilah paused, glancing between her and the door that muted the soirée.

'Is everything okay?' she asked.

Ejem nodded, but a tight nod that said it was not. She watched Delilah's concern war with the promise of fun on the other side of the door. Delilah's movements, a particular twist in her shoulders, the way she clenched her fist, an angled tilt of her head, suddenly brought to Ejem's mind the osu woman on the bus. Something must have crossed her face because Delilah lifted a furtive, self-conscious hand to pat her hair into place – right where an identifying scar would have been if a government midwife had scored it into her head when she was six months old, and then refreshed it on return visits every two years until she turned eighteen. That practice was the extent of Ejem's osu knowledge. Her people lived side by side with the osu and they knew nothing of each other.

Looking at Delilah's box, it occurred to Ejem that an osu girl – if she were clever enough, audacious enough, in possession of impossibly thick hair – could take her most prized possession – say, a fine carved box that had been in the family for many generations – and sneak away in the middle of the night. She could travel farther than she had ever been in her life, to a city where no one knew her. And, because she was clever, she could slip seamlessly into the world of the people she knew so well because she'd had to serve them all her life.

Before the thought could take hold, the uncertainty in Delilah's face was replaced by an artificial sweetness, and she patted Ejem's shoulder, saying, 'Rest well, then,' before escaping into the party.

Ejem was awoken at dawn by the last of the revelers leaving. She stayed in her apartment till eight, then took advantage of Odinaka's open-door policy to enter her benefactor's apartment. If she hadn't been there herself, she would never have believed it had been filled with partiers the night before. In three hours, someone, or several someones, had transformed the wreckage of fifty guests – Ejem remembered at least two spilled wineglasses and a short man who'd insisted on making a speech from an end table – back into the clean, modern lines preferred by one of the wealthiest women in the world. A woman who apparently collected debris, like her. She wasn't exactly sure what she wanted to say to Odinaka – she couldn't childishly complain that one of the guests had insulted her – but she felt injured and sought some small soothing.

She found Odinaka lounging in her bed, covers pulled to her waist.

'Did you enjoy yourself, Ejem? I saw you talking to Aju. He just left, you know.' She wiggled her brows.

Well. Ejem couldn't exactly condemn him now. 'We had an interesting conversation,' she said instead.

' "Interesting," she says. I know he can be difficult. Never mind what he said.'

Odinaka pressed the intercom and requested a breakfast tray, then began to recap the night, laughing at this and that event she didn't realize Ejem hadn't been there to see.

After ten minutes, she pressed the intercom again. 'Where is my tray?' she demanded, a near shout.

Catching Ejem's expression, she rolled her eyes. 'Don't you start as well.'

Ejem opened her mouth to defend the osu women, but shut it just as quickly, embarrassed not only by the unattractive revolutionary bent of what she'd almost said, but also because it felt so much like a defense of herself.

'You are just like Doreen,' Odinaka continued. 'Look, I employ an army of those women. They have a job and they need to do it. You remember how that goes, right?' Odinaka turned on the television. A commercial advertised a family getaway that included passes to a textile museum where the children could learn how cloth was made. Ejem recalled a documentary she'd seen in school that showed the dismal dorms to which unclaimed women were relegated, the rationed food, the abuse from guards, the 'protection' that was anything but. It had been meant to instill fear of ending up in such a place, and it had worked.

When the program returned, Odinaka turned up the volume until it was clear to Ejem she had been dismissed.

Ejem decided that her first foray in her new cloth would be to visit Doreen in her shop. Doreen would know just what to say to ease the restless hurt brewing inside her. She may even know enough of Delilah's history to put Ejem's runaway suspicions to rest. Doreen had invited her to visit the bookstore many times – 'You can't stay in here forever. Come. See what I've done. See what an unclaimed woman can build on her own.'

Wearing self-cloth in the safety of Odinaka's building was one thing. Ejem dawdled in front of the mirror, studying the softness of her stomach, the firm legs she'd always been proud of, the droop of her breasts. She picked up the cloth and held it in front of her. Much better. She secured it in a simple style, mimicking as best as she could the draping and belting of the sophisticated women she'd encountered.

For the first time in her adult life, no one stared at her. When she gathered the courage to make eye contact with a man on the sidewalk and he inclined his head respectfully, she almost tripped in shock. It was no fluke. Everyone – men and women – treated her differently, most ignoring her as yet another body on the street. But when they did acknowledge her, their reactions were friendly.

Ejem felt the protective hunch of her shoulders smooth itself out, as though permission had been granted to relax. She walked with a bounce in her step, every part of her that bounced along with it shielded by the cloth. Bound up in fabric, she was the freest she'd ever felt.

Ejem was so happy that, when she saw a familiar face, she smiled and waved before she remembered that the bearer of the face had disowned their friendship some months ago. Chidinma gave a hesitant wave in return before she approached Ejem, smiling.

'You're covered! You're claimed! Turn around; let me see. Your wife-cloth is so fine. I'm upset you didn't invite me to the claiming ceremony.'

The words were friendly but the tone was strained, their last exchange still echoing in the air.

'There wasn't a ceremony. There was nothing to invite you to.'

Chidinma's smile faded. 'You don't have to lie. I know I was awful to you; I'm sorry.'

'No, really, there wasn't.' Ejem leaned closer, yearning to confide, to restore their former intimacy. 'It's self-cloth. I covered myself.'

It took Chidinma a moment to absorb this. Then she bristled, pulling back any lingering affection. Her smile went waxy and polite.

'You must be very happy with your husband.'

'Chidinma, I don't have a husband. I'm covering myself.'

Chidinma's look turned so vicious that Ejem stepped back, bumping into a man who excused himself.

'Are you, now? A self-cloth, is it? Someone from a good family like yours? I don't believe it.' Unlike Ejem, Chidinma didn't lower her voice, earning startled glances from passersby. Ejem shushed her.

'Oh, are you ashamed now? Did something you're not entirely proud of?'

When Ejem turned to leave, Chidinma snatched her by the cloth. Now she whispered, 'You think you're covered, but you're still naked. No amount of expensive "self-cloth" – how ridiculous! – will change that.'

It was a spiteful and malicious thing to say, meant to hurt, and it did. Ejem tried to pull her cloth from her old friend's fist, but Chidinma didn't let go. She continued, her voice cracking with tears.

'You don't get to be covered without giving something up; you don't get to do that. It's not fair. After everything I did for you, it's not fair.'

Chidinma cried openly now and Ejem used the opportunity of her weakened grip to twist away, near tears herself.

It had been easy, Ejem thought, in the opulence of Odinaka's house, to forget that they were breaking laws. Easy, too, to clink glasses night after night. What had some woman given up so that Ejem could have this cloth? Was she a weaver by choice or indentured, deemed past her prime and burdened to earn the care of the state? The fabric felt itchy now, as though woven from rough wire.

Ejem hurried back the way she had come, to the safety of Odinaka's building. On the verge of panic, she fumbled with the keys to her apartment and let herself in. Once inside, she leaned against the door and slid to the floor, head to knees, catching her breath. She felt... something, that made her look around, and that's when she saw the osu woman standing in the corner. Her skin was light, almost blending into the dusky beige of the wall, her scar a gristly, keloided mass on the side of her head. She appeared to be Ejem's age or older. She held a bottle of cleaning solution and a rag. She was naked.

It was clear by the hunch of her shoulders and the wary look in her eye that it was not a nakedness she enjoyed. How long had it been since Ejem had carried that very look on her own face? How long since she'd felt shame so deep she'd nearly drowned in it?

The day she'd lost her father-cloth, she'd pleaded with her father, fought him as he'd attempted to rip the fabric away. Her mother had cried to her to bear it with some dignity, but Ejem had gone mindless. When her father had finally taken all of the cloth, uncurling her fingers to snatch even the frayed strip she'd held on to, Ejem had curled into herself, making a cover of her appendages. Each day since had been a management of this panic, swallowing it deep in her belly where it wouldn't erupt.

The osu woman nodded to Ejem, then slipped through a panel in the wall and disappeared. The panel slid back into place soundlessly, and when Ejem went to the wall she could feel no seam. She clawed at it, bending and breaking her nails, trying to force a way in. Finding no entry from her side, she pounded and called out, seeking a welcome.

Lesley Nneka Arimah was born in the UK and grew up in Nigeria and wherever else her father was stationed for work. Her stories have been honoured with a National Magazine Award, a Commonwealth Short Story Prize and an O Henry Award. Her work has appeared in the *New Yorker*, *Harper's*, *McSweeney's*, *GRANTA* and has received support from the Elizabeth George Foundation and MacDowell. She was selected for the National Book Foundation's 5 Under 35 and her debut collection *What It Means When a Man Falls from the Sky* won the 2017 Kirkus Prize, the 2017 New York Public Library Young Lions Fiction Award and was selected for the New York Times/PBS book club, among other honours. Arimah is a 2019 United States Artists Fellow in Writing. She lives in Las Vegas and is working on a novel about you. 'Skinned' was first published in *McSweeney's Quarterly Concern*, Issue 53.

The Wall

Meron Hadero

When I met Herr Weill, I was a lanky ten-year-old, a fish out of water in — —, Iowa, a small college town surrounded by fields from every direction. My family had moved to the United States a few weeks earlier from Ethiopia via Berlin, so I knew no English, but was fluent in Amharic and German. I'd speak those sometimes to strangers or just mumble under my breath to say what was on my mind, never getting an answer until the day I met Herr Weill.

I was wearing jeans with a button-down, a too-big blazer and a clip-on tie, waiting in line during what I'd later come to know as a typical mid-'80s Midwest community potluck, with potato salad, pasta salad, green bean casserole, bean salad casserole, tuna pasta salad casserole, a good three-quarters of the dishes on offer incorporating bacon and crushed potato chips and dollops of mayonnaise. The Norman Borlaug Community Center had welcomed us because one of the local bigwigs had been in the Peace Corps in his student days, and he'd cultivated an interest in global humanitarianism. He'd heard of the new stream of refugees leaving communist dictatorships in the Third World, found us through the charity that had given us housing in Berlin, and arranged for the NBCC to orient us, get us some new used clothes and a place to live. They also invited us to Sunday meals, which were the best ones of my week.

On this particular Sunday, I'd walked into the recreational room transformed by paper cutouts of pumpkins and bundled ears of multicolored corn. Cotton had been pulled thin across the windows, and dried leaves pressed in wax paper taped to the wall. Beneath a banner (which I couldn't read) was a plastic poster of a woman with a pointed black hat on her head, her legs straddling a broom, haunting grimace-bearing missing teeth, as if I didn't already feel afraid and alienated in that space. Next to this monstrosity stood a very benign-looking real-life man with a wool scarf and wool coat, who wiped away a bead of sweat as he eyed, then looked away from, then eyed again a pretty woman across the room who was picking through a basket of miniature candy bars.

In German I said to no one in particular, 'Why doesn't he just talk to her?' Nodding at the man with the wool coat, I continued, 'What's he waiting for, permission from his mother?'

Then, from a deep voice behind me, I heard in German: 'There was a woman in my life once. I looked at her the same way.'

When this stranger spoke these words, I recalled the moment a few months back in West Berlin when I was playing soccer with Herman and Ismail, two Turkish brothers who lived on Friedrichstrasse next door to me. Our improvised playground was this plot close to the Berlin Wall where someone had tied a piece of yarn between two old halogen lamps, a makeshift goalpost. Sometimes I'd aim not for those feet between the metal posts but far beyond the Wall. This was in defiance of my mother's strict command to stay away from 'that horror of a serpent'. Wasteful and risky, she called it when I'd told her twice before that I'd sacrificed a soccer ball to the GDR. She was wrong to worry that I'd get in trouble for my antics – I never did. But she was right that I'd been wasteful. We had nothing as it was, and the embarrassment of buying a toy must have been infuriating to her because strangers slandered her with cries of 'welfare woman' and 'refugee scum' when she walked down the street anyway, just to get groceries or some exercise, and when they saw her carrying something as frivolous as a soccer ball, they'd shout louder, with more spit in their breaths and more rage in their eyes.

I knew this, I'd even witnessed this, but for some reason I couldn't help that sometimes, after running circles in the tiny paved playground that pressed against the barricade, I'd visualize this little grounded balloon between my feet soaring to the other side of that imposing wall that seemed to challenge my very sense of freedom, and so I'd close my eyes and kick hard. Herman and Ismail could never – or would never – clear the hurdle, but I'd done it twice already, and the third time I launched the ball just over the barbed wire, I heard a loud grunt from somewhere beyond, and saw the ball come soaring back toward us. I caught it and was stunned. Herman and Ismail yelled at me to send it over again, but I knew it would have broken my heart some if we'd kicked it back and never had it returned. I'd have held tight to hope, I'd have gone back to the spot and waited, I'd have lingered in the playground anticipating a reply, whether or not another ever came. So I convinced Herman and Ismail that we should retire our game, and to make sure of it I put a pin through the ball and let out the air.

This is how I felt standing in the potluck line that October day, looking at the man looking at a woman, hearing this response in German said back to me, the first words I'd understood in this new country spoken by anyone other than my parents: 'There was a woman in my life, once. I looked at her the same way,' the man had said in German, and I replayed this in my mind as I stood there frozen, not daring to say a thing, holding on to my words like I had held that returned ball on the playground.

Johannes Weill went ahead and introduced himself and said everyone just called him Herr Professor Weill or simply Herr Weill because he once was a dean at the college that had won some big international award, and so it stuck. He told me I was famous in town, too. I pointed at myself, wondering what he'd heard. 'You're one of the Ethiopian refugees, right?' Herr Weill asked, then said: 'I've been waiting to meet you. The whole town has been talking.' I nodded, just beginning to trust in this conversation, in the sincere interest of his tone, in his perfect German, in which he continued, 'To answer your question, the man in the wool coat is trying to think of a way to impress the girl, of course.'

'Stringing together a sentence might be a good start,' I suggested. 'His opener is obvious. As she's picking through the basket of candy, ask her what kind of chocolate she likes.'

Herr Weill took off his round glasses and squinted in a way that severely exaggerated the already-deep lines that crossed his face. He held his glasses up to the light, like he had to make sure that I was real and not a speck on his lens or something, and after this pause he replied, 'It's not always easy to find the right words, you know.'

'Maybe you just have to know the right language,' I said.

'Well, if you don't learn English soon, you'll end up like that man in the wool coat, with no way to say what's on your mind or in your heart, except to some old German guy you meet waiting for spaghetti and ham-balls,' he said.' And that doesn't sound like a good way to spend a childhood.'

'Yeah, I'm working on it,' I said.

'I could teach you English.'

'Then you must not know,' I said. The part I didn't say was 'just how poor we are'.

By now I was taking modest spoonfuls from the big Tupperware containers so as not to show just how poor we were. Not to overstate how eager I was for spaghetti and ham-balls, I pursed my lips to hide my watering mouth, and turned away hoping he wouldn't hear the faint rumbling of my stomach.

I finally decided to take bacon that was in strips *and* in rounded patties.

'It's true,' Herr Weill said. 'I didn't teach languages. I was a professor in the arts, but I do know how to teach.'

'But a tutor costs money, and the problem is...'

'A money issue?' he asked and waited, but I didn't respond.

'You'd be doing me a favor,' he said. 'It has been ages since I've spoken German to someone face to face – spoken German to anyone at all. It would be quite nice to have a new friend to talk to.'

I turned to face him. A friend, he'd said, and I nearly repeated him. 'I would like a friend to talk to as well,' I confessed, unable to stop myself from smiling openly now. We shook on the deal, and I bowed slightly in the Ethiopian way as I said, 'Nice to meet you, Herr Weill.'

I'd go to Herr Weill's on Mondays, Wednesdays and Fridays after school. During our early conversations, it was a relief to land on his doorstep after the six hours in a school where no one understood anything about me. My silence, my inability to grasp the very words being said in class, including my own name – mispronounced by the teacher taking the roll. The pungent food I brought for lunch that I ate with my hands. My solitary play at recess that usually involved creative projects with flowers, rocks, wood, whatever I collected from the patch of wilderness on the edge of the playground. My need for expression took on non-verbal forms in those thirty minutes of freedom outdoors. I contributed nothing to the class discussions and understood almost nothing as well, except during our math hour (what a short hour) – my favorite subject, that universal language. Math and art, the only things I cared about. After these exhausting days, I'd walk the mile of country road to Herr Weill's tidy brick house, and it mattered that he always seemed pleased to see me.

Before I went up the walkway that perfectly bisected his perfectly manicured lawn, I'd always straighten my coat, tuck in my shirt and inspect my shoes. He'd greet me in a suit and wing-tipped shoes, hold out his right hand for a handshake while his left arm was held behind his back, like he was greeting a dignitary. His wispy white hair was always parted in the middle in an unwavering line from which thin strands were combed toward his ears. When those strands would flop as he was talking excitedly, shaking his head and index finger while making a point, he'd simply smooth his hair back down once he'd said his piece, that meridian re-emerging just so. He had an unfussy home: no phone, sturdy furniture, lots of these framed silhouette paintings hanging on the walls. He'd set out tea and bread, cheese and meats, and he always made me a to-go box to bring home to my mother. He was well regarded in town, and so my parents quickly warmed to the idea of these meetings, and especially the free English lessons. Whenever I asked my parents a question about English, they'd say, 'That's one to remember for Herr Professor.' Herr Weill and I would usually meet for about two hours. My mother didn't have to worry about finding a sitter or some inexpensive after-school activity for me three days a week. Herr Weill was a blessing, she always said. Father wasn't particularly religious, but he agreed. Herr Weil was a blessing.

We worked through a basic English textbook that had a cartoon of a red schoolhouse with a big sun shining down actual rays of wavy lines, something any preschooler could have drawn, if he had no imagination. We sat with this workbook for an hour and spent the rest of the time speaking German. At first, I was surprised by how much I had to say. With both my parents spending long hours at work cleaning the chemistry lab by day and applying to training programs at night, and with no one to talk to in my neighborhood or at school, I had filled my days with so much silence that my time with Herr Weill was an unexpected outpouring.

Herr Weill didn't reveal very much that first day, but opened up just to tell me he had been a refugee once, too, and had left home when he was a teenager because a war scattered his whole family. He spoke slowly and said little, but it was also an outpouring, I could tell. From then on, we talked often about these things, like conflict, violence, war, fleeing from it and the way it makes you tired and confused whether you're running or still. We talked about scars, invisible and visible, instant and latent ones, all real. How hard it is not to keep losing things because of conflict, even once it's far away, miles or years away, and yet how life fills up with other things all the while. At the end of that visit, he said, 'It's a relief to be able to chat with someone around here about something other than Chuck Long,' whom I'd never even heard of anyway.

The second time I visited Herr Weill, he gave me a leather journal so I would always have someone to talk to, if only the blank page. I wrote in German so that I could show it to Herr Weill if he ever asked to see it. I was always jotting down notes about my life, about the things I'd encounter and wanted to think about, conversations that were mostly reflections of what I longed to say and hear.

Li is from China. I've been sitting next to her in the back of the room ever since last week when we were the only people in the class without costumes for Halloween. She told me a secret: her family fled from the first country, and she asked me if I knew what she meant and I did. I told her I even knew what it meant to flee from the second country, and also to leave the third country, and that made her smile. She has a pretty smile. And she's really good at drawing. And geography. Maybe because she saw me writing in this journal, she gave me a box of pens today. She always has these nice pens she draws with that have little pandas on them. She gave me a whole box. How did she know I love pandas? Her English is worse than mine. When she handed me the pens, she said something like, 'Your book'. I tried to say, 'Thanks, pandas are my favorite animals', but she didn't respond. Maybe underneath, it really went like this, or could have:

Me: *How's everything?*

Li: *I'm fine, how are you?*

Me: *I'm fine. I've just been writing in this journal that my best friend gave me.*

Li: *What are you writing about?*

Me: *Oh, just about life and love and things like that.*

Li: *Wow! I brought you pens so you can keep writing in your book.*

Me: *Thanks, pandas are my favorite animals!*

Li: *Mine, too!*

Me: *I'll dedicate this journal to you.*

Li: *I'd like that very much.*

Later, I will try to tell Li that Herr Weill is taking me to the college library. It will be closed for Veteran's Day, but he has a 'ritual' to go every year the day before on 10 November. He thinks I might like it there, too.

Every 10 November Herr Weill would go to the college library to see what he called his German collection. Before we met, this was the only German he heard all year. He'd read German books out loud, and it was the only German he spoke all year, too. Herr Weill and I took a bus to the library. The roof of the bus had these little gold stars painted on to it, and I thought that was a fine touch. Unlike in Berlin, you could look up at night from any point in this town and see the stars anyway, but still, it was nice to be reminded of a clear night sky on a cold morning.

Herr Weill knew everyone at the library, and they all came over to say hi and see how he was doing. He introduced me to the research librarians and other staff. They took us to a very small room made of glass that reminded me of an elevator I'd once seen in Berlin. The room had two chairs in it and shelves for books. He gave the research librarian a stack of bits of paper with numbers and letters and, about a half hour later, the librarian rolled a cart over to our little room. The cart was full of books, maps, newspapers, photographs, most of them dusty as if they hadn't been touched all year.

We spent the whole day there with these items. So we could keep up our energy, Herr Weill snuck in breakfast, lunch sandwiches, a snack and a light supper. I wrote down everything I could about what I saw in our glass room because it was such a standout day. I saw:

Café Elektric, *a silent film with Marlene Dietrich and with no ending because it is said to be lost. Herr Weill thinks the end was later lost in the war because that's the nature of war, to leave stories incomplete and rob us of our resolutions (we also listened to Marlene Dietrich sing in The Blue Angel).*

The Threepenny Opera *by his 'namesake by coincidence', Kurt Weill, also a refugee. The song I remember was about mercy being more important than justice and Herr Weill said he listened to it every year to see if he'd come any closer to deciding whether or not this was true, and, if it was true, what it required of him or what it eased in him, so he said.*

Poems by the poet Rilke.

A few pages of *Zen and the Art of Archery, which Herr Weill had been reading a few pages at a time for years, each year. We took turns reading aloud. He said Zen doesn't believe in language, so it's best to give the pages space, months, years to breathe. He folded over the top, a tiny bend marking where we would pick up next November.*

News clips from 10 November 1938, because of the treacherous anniversary of Kristallnacht. Herr Weill says it's important to acknowledge an anniversary, even the ones that mark tragedy. This was around the time he left Germany and became a refugee, which I can tell he doesn't like to speak about. He said very little about 1938 except that some things we can't help but remember, and some we must struggle to forget. I forgot to ask him which things are which.

Old maps and new ones because Herr Weill said that the borders can change on you, so you have to keep watch, keep checking in. Through the maps, I learned some more about Herr Weill and my old home:

Herr Weill was born in 1920, not in Berlin, but in a suburb. By the time he was two months old, the city had grown at least three times because someone moved some lines on a map. So he was born just outside of Berlin and grew up in Berlin, having lived in the same house all his childhood. I saw the old map of Germany in 1919 and in 1920. He called it something else, Weimar.

He pointed out the borders of the Jewish ghetto that he said had walls of its own when Germany was called something else, the Third Reich, but he didn't call it that himself, he said.

We looked at a map of Germany after World War Two with Berlin in the eastern part of the country. This was before the USSR built the Wall, but still there was West Berlin with borders around it, a floating dot in the Communist bloc. Herr Weill said, 'It's a very uneasy thing to live life surrounded by enemies.' I knew this to be true.

A satellite map outlining the wall built in 1961. From this point of view, it had none of the order I always associated with the Wall.

On a modern map of West Berlin, I pointed out where our studio was situated in the shadow of the Wall on the Western side, which looked the same as the shadow that fell on the East. I pointed out where Herman and Ismail had lived. I found the general location of our playground, and also where I liked to sit by the Spree and watch the boats when I was in the East and where I liked to sit by the Spree and watch the boats in the West just like I liked to watch the boats when we went on vacation to the banks of Lake Tana.

I will always remember the way Herr Weill quoted me back to myself after that day, saying, 'You say you lived with your family "in the shadow of the Wall on the Western side, which looked the same as the shadow that fell on the East". In this, you have pointed out the main aspect of a wall that these damn architects never seem to grasp: no matter which side you're on, its shadow is cast on you.' He'd say it at random times, and reflect on those words in a way that made me feel understood.

At the end of our visit to the college library, Herr Weill wished me a happy eve of Armistice Day, his favorite holiday, marking the end of World War One, a 'war to end all wars, a day that for a moment must have seemed to promise eternal peace, for a while'. I asked, 'Why celebrate a day that was a lie, there was no armistice to end all wars?' but Herr Weill replied, 'Even if a promise isn't kept, it doesn't mean there has been a lie.' He said we'd do this again next year, and being let in to this annual ritual gave me the feeling we'd be friends for a long time. Before I left, Herr Weill invited me and my parents to lunch at his home on 11 November, but I told him my father didn't have the day off and my mother wanted me to help mend the winter clothes we'd been given while we were still wearing our fall clothes.

14 November, sunny, freezing, so cold that recess is getting shorter so we've been playing inside. I started to pass notes to Li in the back of the room:
Monday: Do you like me? Yes, No, Maybe
    Li answered by drawing a doodle of a cat sleeping on a chair.
Tuesday: Want to play after study time? Yes, No, Maybe (circle one)
    Li answered by drawing a tic-tac-toe board and putting an x in the middle.

Wednesday: No note (playing it cool)
Thursday: Would you like to share my juice box
   today?
   Li drew a sun with sunglasses on it!
Friday: Can we play tomorrow in the park?
   Li wrote the words to the Pledge of Allegiance.

I couldn't tell if Li and I were growing closer or missing each other. There were few friends in my life. Ismail and Herman had left Germany just before I did, and the only letter I wrote was never forwarded, just returned unopened, wrong address. I couldn't write my friends back home because my parents said it was unsafe to tell them where we'd escaped to. Though I barely talked to Li, she was my closest friend at school. I longed to know her better.

   I brought my heartache to Herr Weill, tentatively. I eased into the subject, asking Herr Weill, 'When I first met you, didn't you say there was a woman you looked at once with longing?' He lifted his brow, and revealed that, sure, he'd loved a woman once. They were neighbors in Berlin. He was shy, she was shy. He'd carry her groceries, walk her to school sometimes, tried to show her he was a dependable rock in her life, and he had it all planned out in his mind: when he graduated from high school, started a job, and had enough money to take her out in style, then he'd ask her to dinner. But the war happened, and it didn't end in time. They both walked into the war, never reconnecting. She was always good to him. Her name was Margareta.

I asked him, 'If you never married her, did you ever marry anyone else?'

'Almost once, but it fell apart. Then another time almost, but it slipped through my fingers. That seemed like as many chances as I was going to get. But I every so often wonder about Margareta, just like I wonder about many things from back home that eluded me,' he admitted.

'Do you regret not pursuing her?' I asked him.

'You see,' he said, 'one always regrets a lack of courage. In one form or another, that's probably the only kind of regret anyone ever has.'

'So you tried to find her again later?' I pressed, testing my own feelings about Li against his answers and experience.

'No, I haven't tried to find her yet,' he said. I didn't feel the need to tell him the obvious, that forty-five years seemed long enough to wait. But I was shy, too, so I could understand where he was coming from, which made me even more upset. I decided that I'd need to learn from this, to be bolder than he was in matters of the heart, and I came up with a name for my plan to win Li ASAP: Operation Panda Margareta, which was both my favorite animal, the animal I imagined Li also loved, and the name of the woman Herr Weill had once loved.

I talked to Herr Weill about it and he seemed charmed, understood that something as monumental as Operation Panda Margareta would need to be dramatic, carefully planned, and very strategically implemented. The next time I saw him I showed him my idea, which he thought seemed adequately heroic:

OPERATION PANDA MARGARETA
9:15: Sneak into the Principal's office while Principal
is out for his daily smoke/walk
9:16: Play the Jackson 5's 'ABC' over the PA
9:17: Read a poem for Li
9:19: Run!

I worked on the plan on my own, especially writing the poem, which took time since my English was still halting. A couple of weeks later, I was leaving school to visit Herr Weill and go over last-minute details for Operation Panda Margareta, recite the poetry, test out the cassette player my dad had loaned me, and go over the book I'd checked out from the library on operating a PA system, when I noticed Thomas Henry – sweet, quiet farm kid – come down the front steps of the school, walk up to Li, and, without saying a thing, put his arm around her in a familiar way, like he'd certainly done it before. Behind his ear he had a panda pen, and my heart was sinking. I fumbled for the poem in my pocket, and I almost did what I had meant to do, read these words to Li, declare my feelings. When Thomas and Li walked by, I tried to catch Li's gaze, but I couldn't quite keep it.

I stopped writing in my notebook after this, and just before winter break Li began sitting with Thomas and his friends up by the front of the room. I joined a soccer club and cut back on my visits to Herr Weill's. I made all kinds of excuses, but the truth is as my English improved, other barriers came down, too, just like Herr Weill predicted. I was discovering more about my classmates, that it turned out they also found it fun to watch the magic tricks that Benny the crossing guard practiced on his breaks and also liked playing in the cleared fields surrounding town. They pranked me by teaching me dirty words but telling me the wrong definition (for about a week, I thought *cabbage* was an insult, *artichoke* a sin to say). I pranked them by showing them sophisticated, 'worldly' ways to dance and shop and roller-skate that were ridiculous and hilarious and got us all kicked out of a few establishments.

So in this way, Herr Weill and I drifted apart, allowed ourselves to become somewhat untied from each other, and let the ebb and flow of life move us along our own paths. I'd still go by from time to time, after chatting at the community center and making plans to meet some weeks, until eventually, with weekend matches to play, I stopped going to those Sunday potlucks, too. When I did come over, Herr Weill would put out meats, cheeses and breads as always, and I allowed myself to imagine he did this whether I came or not, set out this spread every afternoon, that he wasn't going out of his way for me on these haphazard visits. By the spring, my parents decided it was time for us to move again, this time to move toward something: a new job for my father pulling us away. A better job, no longer washing lab instruments but now getting training in a hospital in a town that American doctors avoided. And so we packed our bags again, I hoped for the last time.

Herr Weill and I wrote letters for the first few months after this, but then I guess I just couldn't keep up, or just didn't. The letters piled up, four unanswered ones from Herr Weill that I'd only read quickly, meant to answer but hadn't, life becoming something else by now.

We nearly met again, almost, just after 9 November 1989, when suddenly and unexpectedly the Berlin Wall fell. My first thought upon hearing the news was where were Ismail and Herman, and maybe they could reclaim our lost soccer balls. My second thought was did Herr Weill see the news and what did he think/do/say? I tried to look up Herr Weill in the phonebook, but he still didn't have a number listed, so I told my parents what I wanted to do and they reluctantly let me take the car to visit him the next day, 10 November. I managed to get to the library before it closed. I went to Herr Weill's usual desk but he had left. When I asked, the librarian said Herr Weill had come by for just a short visit and I'd missed him by hours. I requested that old copy of *Zen and the Art of Archery* and saw he'd gone through a few more pages, advanced six unobtrusive folds since the time we'd read this book.

I retraced a path I'd walked so many times, driving that road through the fields and wooded brush. I drove right by his house at first, looking for a large home, circling back, puzzling over how modest it actually was. The paint was faded but the mailbox was new. The lawn was strewn with leaves, some soggy and patted down and some fresh atop that cover, like he hadn't cleared the yard in weeks, maybe all season. It was too late to ring the bell, I told myself. It would have been awkward to visit unannounced then, and I realized I hadn't worked out what I'd have said, anyway. I could sleep in the car and knock in the morning. But it was hard to sleep that night for some reason, and I found myself clearing his lawn with my bare hands of all those messy leaves and filling up his mulch bin. I finished just after dawn, then stayed to pull the tiny weeds that had just sprouted up in the cracks on his pathway leading to his porch, which already had an American flag flying for Armistice Day ('Armistice Day, flags display,' Herr Weill once said). I drove into the quiet town, the shops on Main mostly closed, yet all with bright red-white-and-blue banners hanging in the still morning. I passed my old school and the community center, circled back down by the college, saw the movie theater and the roller rink, each taking on an aura of reverence that a quiet holiday brings.

I thought I might look up Li and see if her family

had managed to stay still in her second country. She'd have been sixteen, a junior in high school, but I never got the courage for that either. I imagined she was getting ready to go to homecoming with Thomas, maybe thinking about buying him a boutonniere and he asking her what color her dress was so he could find the right corsage. As I was filling up the gas tank to make the trip back, I wondered already if I'd regret not looking for Li and I knew I'd regret not having stopped by to visit Herr Weill, our friendship that I'd once thought would last for years already somehow in the past. At least after clearing his lawn, I'd left him a note, simply the first page in the journal he'd once given me and that I still carried around from time to time. On top of the torn-out page, I wrote: *11/11/89, To my first friend in my fourth country on the event of the end of the Wall. A heartfelt and happy Armistice Day.*

Then, in faded ink and smudged lettering:

15 October 1983:
To Herr Weill: Thanks for this journal. It's terrific.
To Journal: Welcome to my life! Herr Weill is my first friend here so far. We have some things in common and some not:
  My favorite food: wurst with kraut and mustard.
    Also dorro wat or kitfo with injera.
  Herr Weill's favorite: schnitzel because his mother used to make it and it is 'comfort food'.
  My favorite movie: Casablanca, ever since they

*played it at the American Consulate because it
was about refugees.*

*Herr Weill's favorite: Casablanca! He says it's a
story about true friendship.*

*My favorite season: I hate the cold because of the
way it makes you cry, but I love reading next
to a fire.*

*Herr Weill's favorite season: he loves the vigor
of the cold, but he hates the snow, too mushy
when it melts.*

*So what else can this mean but that we both love
the fall?*

Meron Hadero was born in Addis Ababa, Ethiopia, but came to the US as a refugee in her childhood via East and West Germany. Her stories appear in *Best American Short Stories*, *McSweeney's*, *Zyzzyva*, *The Iowa Review*, and others. Her writing is also in *the New York Times Book Review* and the anthology *The Displaced: Refugee Writers on Refugee Lives*. She has been awarded residencies at Yaddo, Ragdale and MacDowell, and holds an MFA from the University of Michigan, a JD from Yale Law School (Washington State Bar), and a BA from Princeton in History. Meron is a recipient of a 2019-2020 Steinbeck Fellowship. 'The Wall' was first published in *McSweeney's Quarterly Concern*, Issue 52.

Sew My Mouth

Cherrie Kandie

My lover can only love me behind drawn curtains. The bed must not creak or the neighbours will hear us. On Friday evening, when her parents come to visit, my lover cannot love me because they want her to marry a man. We all sit at the small, brown, rectangular dining table beneath the high serving-hatch that opens to the kitchen. My lover and I sit on one side, her parents on the other. She sits facing her father, who is tall and meaty. He laughs like a big drum. He eats like a big drum too; his inside is large, empty and hollow. He is shoving big ugali mounds into his mouth.

I think that her mother must know, because mothers see the air that mixes between lovers. Her mother must know because she is studying me like a specimen. She narrows her eyes, tightening her brow at the same time. Crow's feet choke the mole next to her left eye. Her face is lined around the eyes, but is otherwise as smooth and deep brown as a loquat seed. Small greyish bushes peep from beneath her blue headscarf; hers is a good strong hairline, just like her daughter's, one that extends far down into her forehead. I turn to my left, and my lover is making concerted conversation with her father, nodding, smiling, matching his raucous laughter, pouring extra words into the natural silences that occur in conversation, pouring her father wine and more wine until his speech slurs and his light-brown cheeks turn pink and shiny with sweat, until his big-drum laughter grows and grows and threatens to swallow our little matchbox flat.

We are eating ugali and creamed sukuma, with kuku kienyeji that I bought at the butcher's for one thousand shillings. I know that my lover's mother likes avocado, so I bought ten of them, each for forty bob. But my lover's mother does not touch them, and neither does she touch the plate of food that I served her.

When I first met her she was pleasant, jubilant even, because I had found her daughter a place to stay near the university. Over and over again, she had said, 'God bless you'. After seven years, however, her genuine and earnest god-bless-yous had disintegrated into a liquid and guarded hostility, which now seeped through her narrowed eyes as she studied me. Three hours ago she had bustled in, just before my lover's father, a dark-blue mermaid kitenge hugging her hips and flaring at her calves, her hair hidden in a matching scarf, her arms laden with baskets of produce from the farm, hugging and kissing us on the cheeks and saying:

'How are you, my daughters?' 'My daughters, I have brought you cabbage and potatoes and peas...' 'You look well, my daughters...'

My daughters, my daughters – another person would have thought that she loved me like a daughter, but I had known otherwise. I had known because I had learned to unearth true intentions, gleaning them like long translucent bones buried deep within tilapia fish. My lover's mother had not been speaking with her mouth, from which her many *my daughters* had fluttered out. She had been speaking with her eyes, which had refused to surrender to the smile on her mouth.

She is still staring at me, eyes equal parts curious and hostile. I think that perhaps she thinks dreadlocks are unbecoming, even if I have pulled them up into a ladylike bun that make my eyebrows feel unusually high; even if I have clipped Magda's dangling earrings onto my un-pierced earlobes. Perhaps she can tell that the black dress with a pink flower print that I bought for today was bought for today, and that I am not in the habit of wearing dresses. I wonder if she can see, with those narrowed eyes, that the dress is too small, that the fabric is cutting into my armpits, that I am sweating under my arms. The food is growing cold, and white Kimbo droplets begin to float on the soup. My mind is running here and running there, out of breath, offering me one reason or another for this woman not liking me. It is trying to convince me that I do not know what she is thinking, it is running careful circles around the truth, it is telling me that she hates me for reasons I can fix.

But I know. I know what she is thinking even before the curiosity in her eyes evaporates, leaving hard hostility behind; before she flings heavy black tar into the air mixing between my lover and me, before she flattens that tar with a roaring steam-roller, when she turns to my lover, smiling, full lips flattened against gleaming teeth, asking: 'Mami, when you will get a husband? And a nice house?'

The skins of the unwanted avocados shine like my lover's father's light-brown cheeks. He is drunk.

On Friday night, after her parents leave, we hold hands and pretend that we are outside. We walk in Nairobi. Our matchbox flat becomes the large sprawling city. The two bedrooms are the suburbs. We live in the bigger of the suburbs, the one with generous pavements and many trees. We leave home and walk along the corridor, which is the highway to town. The kitchen, found just before we get to town, is Fagi's wooden, Coca-Cola box-shaped shop. We lean through the serving hatch and ask for a one-litre Fanta Orange that we put in a paper bag. We hold hands again. We imagine that Fagi says, 'What a lovely couple!'

Then we get to the Central Business District. The sitting room, which is also the dining room, is the CBD. The wall unit that almost touches the ceiling is the Times Tower. We look up and say: 'How tall!

How long did they take to build that?'

At last we go back to our house in the suburbs after spending the whole day bumping into rough fabric sofas and smooth aluminium matatu chests, into polished wooden stools and grey concrete buildings, into sweaty people and dining chairs with proud long backs, all of these fitting, as if by magic, in the small CBD of our flat. When we get to our bigger room, we lie on the same bed. If our lover's mother were to come in and find us, she would exclaim, 'My daughters!' This time, her mouth would slacken, unable to smile. Her eyes would become round, un-narrowed, because whose arm was whose? Whose skin was whose? Whose leg was whose? Our body parts would be mixed up together like pieces of meat in a stew, in a sufuria without a lid, exposed because the lazy blanket had fallen off in the middle of the night.

The next day, Saturday, Magda is gathering water in her palms and lifting it onto her body. The wide blue-plastic basin is perched on a stool, the whole arrangement a castle chess piece. First she is gathering up only as much as a dog's tongue because the water is cold, then she is gathering up more, then I hear no more water because she is scrubbing, and then I begin to hear larger and louder water as it pours over her body, and the thirsty drain, as it drinks it up. She comes out wrapped in a white towel and asks me if I have seen the nail-cutter, and I want to tell her that it is in the second bedroom, on the desk by the window. Keep your nails short: school rule or *lesbianology*? But this is when Magda's vibrating phone stirs us. It is a text from Thomas, our neighbour, to say that he is at the door. As Magda rushes to dress, I rush to mix the blankets on the bed in the smaller second bedroom, trying to make it look slept in, tossing some of the red towels that clutter the bed into the cupboard, throwing a pair of jeans onto the floor, opening the curtains. Magda and I scamper around our matchbox flat like rats; I think of green rat-poison pellets floating in a glass of Fanta Orange. I want to lie down for a bit, and cry for a bit, but I hear the sound of the door opening and I hear Magda saying loudly: 'Thomas! Mambo!'

And thus, Thomas has fractured our gentle reverie. Magda is louder now, fussing over him, very much like her mother, 'Sasa wewe, what will we cook for you? Do you want tea? How is job?' Her crotchet-braid weave bobs as she rushes from the kitchen to the sofa to the dining table, reheating food and setting a stool before him. 'Tom, dear, how much chilli do you like in your food?' – 'Maji ama Coke?' – 'I'm sorry that this is taking so long!'

Thomas glows under Magda's uxorial light; he is smiling as he watches her shuffle about. Madga smells like Nivea body lotion, good food and three fat future children, two boys and one girl. Thomas, twenty-nine, wants to be with her, would marry her, on his thirty-second birthday, at the

Holy Family Minor Basilica in town, him dapper in a black suit, her veiled in all-white, his family on the pews on the right and hers on those on the left. I know all this because I trawled through the Whatsapp messages he sent Magda, all of them unanswered, arranged one after the other like rectangular stones on a stepping-stone pathway.

He would marry her, but here I am. I sit quietly on the adjacent sofa. I know how to shrink myself to live. My father taught me how to make myself smaller. First he taught my mother, then me, then my three little bald sisters, one after the other, each of us with big-big eyes yearning to be enough for a man who wanted a son but got four daughters, each next one with rounder eyes and a bigger forehead, foreheads made to look even bigger because any trace of hair was promptly shaved off. To look neat for school, my father had said; to keep boys away, my father had also said. My mother promised me hair as soon I finished high school. I and my egg head had made ourselves so small that our father could not see us. I know now that if I make myself small enough to almost disappear, I will be left alone to live.

But Magda swells up, she is swelling up now, big like her big drum father, big like her afro weaves, hiding herself under loud layers, showy like her fabulous mother. When her parents are far away in Eldoret, when Thomas leaves, when I have fallen asleep, and when all the lights are off, my lover goes into the smaller bedroom. There, with the steady, solitary and painful focus of a chicken trying to lay an egg, she peels off all those layers. Perched on her red towels and locked away from me, she prays, shakes, and rakes razors across the skin of her inner thighs.

There is nothing like Magda's hair. It is the darkest of clays, which she moulds into many shapes. Buns, braids, cornrows, weaves, mixtures of two or three or all of these, shrunken tiny afros or picked spherical ones, wigs, hats, sometimes with her front hair showing, and, finally, cloth hair – scarves twisted and bunned at the back. My hair is weak and fine, and can only grow long in dreadlocks, and even then, it never is voluminous. So Magda's hair is even more beautiful to me, the good strong hairline, the many shapes, the balls of shed hair like cotton strewn all over the dresser. The only thing that I like more than her hair is her skin. It is darkest between her thighs, and there, on each side, I find short, black and precise scars, arranged like gills.

On TV, a politician says that there is no space for gays in Kenya. Thomas says: 'I support him. Can you even imagine a *dick* in your *ass*?' He takes a slow sip from the glass of Coke that Magda has set out for him, and licks his lips. With a prodding half-smile, he adds in a lower voice, staring straight at Magda, 'But I *support* the L. That one I most definitely *support*.' He is the kind of man from whose mouth sentences slide easily, ropes curling into nooses encircling women's waists. My jaws grow hot as I imagine him masturbating to *lesbian porn*. He adds, 'But how many letters are there in that thing again?'

There is a stilted pause in the conversation. There is too much to ignore, even for Magda. Perhaps she is thinking that he knows. What would follow then would be to wonder what the implications of his knowing would be. In the end, Magda recovers from the brazenness of it all, strangling the too-long pause with a big laugh, flinging it under her loud layers, almost screaming-laughing, and saying, not even sarcastically: 'Thomas, you are so funny! Oh my gosh! *How many letters are there in that thing!*'

Marionettes are sinister because they are controlled by strings that lead up to the Devil. If I were to pinch a normal person, they would frown or slap my hand away or cry out or pinch me back. But if I were to pinch a marionette, its empty eyes would just stare back at me, wooden and smiling, dancing and clapping.

Magda turns to me laughing, repeating: '*How many letters are there in that thing*! Don't you think that's so funny?' Her eyes are clear and round, her mouth stiff and stretched into a smile, straight teeth arranged dutifully, kernels of white maize on a cob. Her voice is thick brown, millet porridge, rich and homely; sugary and buttery, but tinged with something bitter – very likely lemon juice, straight from the lemon.

Underneath puppets' veneers are knives that

will slice your throat in your sleep. White wriggly maggots under a lush and pretty log.

Thomas interjects: 'Magda, you look so pretty when you laugh like that. Let me take a picture of you. Where is your phone? Mine's just gone off.'

I am shrinking, crawling, deeper under the bed, Thomas' words trailing after me. I am thinking of the night months ago when Thomas had banged on the door, speech slurred, *I want to see Magda, I want to see Magda*, how we had put off the lights and tiptoed to the smaller bedroom, waiting under the bed for the banging to stop and for him to leave, how the thick puddle of low-thrum anxiety nestled at the base of my throat had exploded into hiccupping panic as I had heard the door burst open, as I had clung to precious Magda, under the weight of her red towels, the dusty underside of the bed choking the both of us. How my mouth had remained sewn.

The next morning Madga had mopped up the muddy footprints that tracked from the door through the sitting room all the way to the corridor. He had not got to the bedrooms. I had gone out and found a serious fundi with a pencil behind his ear. He had fixed the broken door and added a new grill, with fat metal bars, standing tall and straight like askaris.

On Sunday morning I wake up, and Magda is not next to me. I try to open the door to the second bedroom but it is locked. I feel faint, so I go to the balcony for some fresh air. On the street below, at the bus stop just outside our building, matatus snarl in the dust like wild cats. It is hot. There are hardly any trees or pavements. Then I notice that all the red towels are gone from the hanging line. I rush back to the second bedroom, and through the door I say: 'Magda, are you okay? Open the door, please.'

'Give me some time alone, please.'

Her voice is weak and watery, like strungi, poor people's milkless tea. Worry makes it difficult for me to reply calmly: 'Okay. How much time?'

No response. I coax some more, but not even the watery weakness reappears. I want to bang on the door. I want to scream MagdaMagdaMagda, but the neighbours will hear me. So I sew my mouth. But the trapped Magdas remain at the base of my throat, popping like fried oil. Then they are flowing downwards, still popping, burning the inner walls of my body, shaking me. I think I should cook some tea that I will not drink, because perhaps the smell will calm me down. I am shaking as I cut open the plastic milk packet with a knife, and, halfway through this, the packet slips and bursts on the floor. I drop the knife, I forget the tea, I am sobbing, sinking to the tiled floor, the hems of my heavy cotton sweatpants wetting with milk, like wicks.

When Magda and I had talked about God, she had said: 'You don't understand. It is God who keeps me alive.' I had wondered where I could get some of this God of Magda's. He had sounded like the beef cubes I add to potato stew when it gets too bland.

Still I had not understood. This God business had outgrown me. It was like an old sweater I wore as a child, now too small and scratchy. My God was not gentle like Magda's; my God was like my father, whose house breathed only after he had left. But now, staring at the diamond patterns on the ceiling, crying-convulsing, with milk soaking my scalp, my back, my panties, my legs, I begin to mutter, God please, God please. It is now only me, and Magda, and Magda's good God.

My heavy cotton sweatpants are stubbornly wet, but the milk on my cotton T-shirt is drying and sticky on my back. I am no longer convulsing but I am still sobbing softly, kneeling at the door of the smaller bedroom and trying out each of the keys in the pile I found in a basket on top of the fridge. The sixth turns the lock. The door flings open. The room is dark, the curtains are drawn. There is a smell of zinc. I switch on the light. Magda lies naked on her red towels, her dark thighs a mess of red. I kneel beside her. She is breathing.

But my lover's mother will love her and will crush her. She will take her daughter's heart and crush it between her narrowed eyes, between eyelids heavy and strong with love that cuts with the strength of diamonds. Magda, twenty-seven and weary of this crushing love, will grow louder and bigger to hide her crushed heart. Like an agitated turkey, her feathers will fan out, her face will fill with blood. Later she will think it unfair that a heart should bear this crushing alone. She will make her thighs bleed again. At least this is what I tell myself because even though she is lying there bleeding and barely breathing, I do not want to call her parents without her consent. But mostly, I am afraid that if they take her away, I may never see her again.

It is like she has given birth to the Devil.

I mend her thighs. She leaves after two weeks. In the end, her mother is the person that she goes back to, tail between legs, heart in hands, wanting it soothed. After she cut herself, a quiet voice told me that it was my fault. That it was the thing that mixed up the air in between us that was cutting her. That it had grown too big for the only place in which I could love her. It had become too much, too raucous. It had swallowed us. It had shrunk me. And it had cut her thighs, every year for three years, always a few days after her parents' visit. I stopped meeting her eyes when I changed her bandages twice a day. I stopped talking to her, responding wordlessly to her needs for drinking water, the toilet, bananas, the bhajias fried in a shack directly opposite our building.

I expected her to leave. When the rain went and the sun came, my father did not fret that the rain had gone. It was time for the maize in the fields to ripen. And so, after the scars had healed, like the rain, like a patient discharged, Magda put on her red maxi skirt and left with a small bag.

But the house is heavy with my beloved. I cannot sleep in the bigger bedroom because her hair is on the dresser, not to mention in the smaller bedroom, where she had given birth to the Devil. I sleep on the rough fabric sofa, maroon with gold-thread flowers. I refuse to touch the mixture of towels, blood and red dye in the basin on the balcony. One day I feel that I do not want to see anyone, not a soul, not even a cockroach, ever again. So I call my boss to quit my PR job where I am obligated to wear short grey skirts. He tells me he has already given away my job because I did not show up for three weeks and didn't respond to his calls. I cook and cry. From the sofa, I begin to design websites for a living. When money gets tight, I take up Magda's old job at a DVD shop a few minutes' walk from the flat.

One evening, two months later, I come back home from the DVD shop and know that Magda is back because the towels hang stiff and foul on the balcony, now a dull orange after bleeding out all their dye. I expected that she would leave, and now I accept that she has come back. She comes out of the kitchen. Her hair is gone, cropped close to her scalp. I am not sure whether her cheekbones had always been so high, her eyes so big, her irises so large, floating like cocoa beans in milk. It had been seven years of seeing only her hair.

That night we sleep heads touching, breathing each other, arms around each other. I roll over to face the other side and Magda moves with me, her nose at my nape, her arm still wrapped around me. Even though neither of us had contacted the other, I had spent all this time expecting that she would come back. So I am glad that I no longer have to expect. But I am also stifled by the suddenness of her return. I know that it is the rain's place to come unannounced. But I also know that Nairobi November skies tend to be heavy and cloudy like grey wet blankets, ones that mother spirits wring to drench the city. The question is: is the coming of rain in Nairobi in November expected or unexpected?

It is perhaps a matter of weather in relation to climate. The weather is mercurial: in the morning it wants pink lipstick, and by noon it has decided that today is a red-lipstick day. Some days it ties its arms around me, and other days it cannot meet my eyes. If the weather is a yellow banana peel racked with black scars, then the climate is what is inside. It is the way Magda squeezes my hand under tables when I have sewn my mouth so tightly that I can hardly breathe. It is the certainty that is the great big engine that is her heart: how it runs on butter and Baringo honey, and how it warms me, melting open my stitches.

Therefore, if a particular Nairobi November day

appears sunny from inside the house, then what do we say to someone who goes out to the salon to flat-iron their hair, expecting that the straightness will last for at least a week and a half, and then does not have an umbrella in their bag on the very day that the rain decides to come the way that Jesus said that he would, kinking their expensive straightness? Is the coming of rain in Nairobi in November expected or unexpected? We can say, yes, it is your fault, the rain was expected, this is November, why didn't you have an umbrella, you just go home and style your afro. We can also collect in a corner and decide that no, it is not your fault, the rain was unexpected, it has been sunny for the whole day, imagine, it only decided to rain once you stepped out of the salon, pole sana, let us curse heaven together. There are things that are both expected and unexpected, and the rain is one of these things.

Cherrie Kandie is a Kenyan writer and a senior at college in the United States of America. She also makes short films and enjoys dancing to Lingala (only in her room). 'Sew My Mouth' was first published in *ID Identity: New Short Fiction From Africa* (Short Story Day Africa/New Internationalist 2018).

It Takes A Village Some Say

Ngwah-Mbo Nana Nkweti

Volume 1: Our Girl

I

Don't believe everything you read in the tabloids. We're nothing like the others. We're not The Slick Salikis splashed page to page in the papers; a couple utterly obsessed with living the good life, so concerned with keeping up appearances that we pimped out our own daughter. Fabrications. Rag-sheet revisionist history. All of it. We did our best by Our Girl.

She was eleven years old when we got her, Our Girl. She came to us with a shocking expedited-shipping efficiency after years of adoption delays: endless home studies, background checks, credit checks, health checks – then ding-dong, ding-dong, a child, handily home-delivered. Imported from the motherland. She was bundled up in this sad little polyester coat, the color of off-brand cola – fudgy brown, tasteless, fizzy – utterly useless in warding off the cold and bluster of that winter night. We pulled her shivering frame into the warmth of our home and she scuttled off to an entryway corner – so straight-backed and vigilant between our coat-rack and umbrella stand.

Her guardian, Mrs Dukong, a booming storm cloud of a woman, thundered in behind her. Teeth chattering. Chatter chattering: Hello, hello! It's so cold, so cold. They had just been to Houston, she told us (so warm!) and then on to (so windy!) Chicago. She pronounced the latter 'Qi-cargo', which sounded vaguely like the name of some New Age travelware boutique, a nag champa-scented place specializing in vegan carry-ons for the ashram hermitage set. It was the kind of shop we might have frequented in our East Village heydays; before our vacation fund became the baby fund, before we moved out of the city to a home with a backyard and a swing set and a better school system for our someday children.

'The girl? Call her anything, anything you like,' she said. 'Call me Aunty Gladys. "Mrs Dukong." Hmph. So formal, so formal.'

We were seated in the formal living room. We could see that Aunty Gladys was impressed. She was meant to be. It was our showcase parlor: chandeliered, marbled, credenza-ed; a place where we received guests with a dazzling solicitousness typically the dominion of ambassadors feting visiting state dignitaries. Our Girl sat mutely by the flames of our hearth, while we beamed at her warmly from the comfy remove of a Chesterfield sofa.

'Mrs Du... Aunty Gladys,' we began. 'We're so grateful–'

'Nonsense. It is the girl's family that is grateful,' she answered. 'Grateful that one of you is from Cameroon so she will know her culture. Not grow up like these young girls twerking their makande on television. Godless Americ...' – she stopped to gape silently at the salt and pepper set we made – 'sorry, sorry. The cold has scattered my brains.'

We were suitably understanding. How could we be otherwise? What followed was all courtesy and business. Yes, Our Girl had all the appropriate papers. The girl's parents? Her father, may he rest, would be so honored by this opportunity for his youngest daughter to live in white-man country. Her mother? Back home, with Our Girl's six younger sisters, happy to know that at least one daughter would go to bed each night with more than cold gari in her belly.

This saddened us, this sibling separation, but we couldn't take them all on, could we? We – a chemist, a botanist turned floral stylist – were hardly millionaires. We lived an average middle-class New Jersey 'burb life: a two-story colonial with a three-car drive and ballooning mortgage payments, two car notes paid off, the other, not so much. Our new Aunty understood, took the balance of the $30,000 in fees we had agreed upon, told us it would help them, told us that this was the way it was done 'back home'. One child lifted up and up till they returned and lifted their whole family out of shantytown quartiers, out of thatch huts, out of hollowed and hungry lives.

We nodded in understanding.

Our Girl's family would be our family, we told her.

How could it be otherwise?

II

We were finally a family. Finally! Well, not quite. An adjustment period was to be expected, after all. For weeks, Our Girl roamed our home merely touching things, eyes saucered, while we followed her hopefully with our own. She was fascinated by bling (usage courtesy of a How to Talk to Your Pre-Teen pamphlet, just a coin-toss pick from the multitude of parenting e-books, magazine articles, and podcasts we devoured). Bling: our Le Creuset crystal vases, the gold-leaf lion head knobs of an armoire, even the gleaming touchscreen interface of our chrome Whirlpool washer. We took to wearing our shimmery baubles and finery indoors, pantomiming our movements – exaggerated yawns and back stretches that dingle-dangled bracelets and wristwatches, anything to draw her to us. We craved her approbation. Anxiously laid shiny objects at her feet like penitents. Did she like her new room (kitted out in cotton-candied furls of pink)? Were her patent-leather Mary Janes too tight (the sizes her Aunty Gladys emailed had been as off the mark as that miserable winter coat she had bought the girl)?

In retrospect, it is all a tad embarrassing, that bottomless need for validation. We needed a win; we habitual gold star-earners, merit scholars, six-figure careerists. For years, amongst the Forjin-dams, the Atekwanas, the Bangwanas of our Cameroonian clique, we had been failures, repro-ductive underachievers. In another time, another wife might discreetly have been proffered by some well-meaning village aunty, oh so solicitous about maintaining the family line. Ours was a tribe in which marriage and procreation went hand in hand, peopled by descendants of rural gran-grans accustomed to measuring their worth by number of offspring like so many sacks of cacao. Although Western diplomas brought Western mindsets, remnants of old ways persist.

'Habi white women no sabi born pickin? Habi nah the man who no get bedroom power?' our so-called friends conjectured in whispers as they dandled chubby infants or chomped on oily sese plantain at every born-house but our own. Amongst our New York social set, it was somehow worse; we were the definition of mediocre, an average Joe and Jane. There were our co-op neighbors, the Talbots – childless by choice, a couple who took open-jaw journeys around the globe toting that vegan luggage from Bali to Madagascar, while we watered their fire-escape philodendrons. Then the chef-owners at our favorite bistro, Tomas and Didier, devastated yet resilient after a childhood friend reneged on her promise to be their birth mother, to Easy-Bake-oven their offspring.

But poor, barren Mr and Mrs Saliki were finally a family. Gone from duo to trio. And after nine bumpy, oops-riddled months, we were getting the hang of things with the evidence to prove it: snap-shots on IG, thousands of page views for 'Bringing Up Baby/Bébé/Mtoto/Bimbo', our inter-racial, multicultural, childrearing blog. We had become chronic chroniclers. If alien life forms explored our planet eons from now, there would be irrefu-table proof, found footage of our happy family: at the pumpkin patch, canoodling with mall Santas, attending any number of calendared events at the Children's Museum enrichment series. We were building our own exhibit of sorts: a collection of report cards and other artifacts, often lacquered and laminated, shining, as if under glass.

The corridors of Highland Terrace Middle School were bemusedly circuitous and maple-wooded, we held hands as we Hansel and Greteled our way through this educational IKEA in search of the Principal's Office. We had been called in for a special conference to discuss our precocious child's 'special needs'.

'There you are, Mr and Mrs Saliki.' A secretary sidled up on slipper-heeled feet, ushering us into the cool hush of another wood-paneled chamber where Principal Artemis sat in state behind a huge coffin of a desk. Her brow was pinched behind dark cat's eye glasses. We sat where we were instructed to.

'It's customary to begin these meetings with some pleasantries, with chit-chat,' she said, 'yet the circumstances that led me to call you here are of such a serious nature... well, I can see no other way but to get right to the heart of the matter.'

Here she paused. But we were trained observers, habituated to gathering facts before formulating shaky conclusions. We merely leaned forward to indicate our interest. She seemed taken aback, hesitated a moment, then said:

'Well, your daughter, well... she has done very well here at Highland, in spite of some initial concerns about her ability to adjust to the culture here, our expectations. We make every effort to be inclusive here.'

'Inclusive?' we echoed. Yes, no doubt they thought they were. There were two Indian students from Uttar Pradesh, a half-Czech Latina, as well as ongoing relations with a sister school in Qingdao, China. And yes, there was Our Girl.

'Yes, inclusive,' said Artemis, forging on. 'Progressive, in fact. But even we have our limits. There are some practices that we simply cannot tolerate. Your daughter has been... appropriating... the belongings of others.'

'Appropriating?' one of us queried in confusion.

'You mean stealing?' said the other, attempting to clarify.

'No, no. We have no evidence of that. Well, we've had complaints from other parents. About items. Items gone missing from their homes. Items later noted in her possession.'

'This is ridiculous,' we cried out. 'She's not stealing, so how did she–?'

'Gifts. She says they were gifts. From male students who were interested in her...'

'So all you really know is that a few moon-eyed teenage boys gave her "gifts". And you called us in here for that?!'

We rose in ire.

Her voice rose as well. 'Mr and Mrs Saliki! Please understand. These items were family heirlooms: Dr Donovan's ruby tie-clip; a diamond clasp passed down in the Connellys' family for generations. Worth thousands of dollars. Priceless.'

'Where are these items? Certainly not in our home.'

'I don't imagine she would just leave these things hanging around in plain sight. Would she? Your daughter is a very clever girl.'

'Not by this account,' we replied.

'But there's more. Some of the young men. Well, they say she does things, sexual things, for these items.'

'They say, they say,' we parroted, cawing with bitter mirth, well versed in the cutting power of whispers made truth.

We were done then. Up and out of the room. Of course only after we had tossed off the obligatory threats to call our attorneys, cried foul regarding Our Girl's token race status, but really all we wanted was to take her home and make sure she was safe. You see, she was damaged when we got her, Our Girl. Something Aunty Gladys had neglected to mention, lest we contract some 'buyer's remorse'. Imagine! It had come out in family therapy. There was an uncle, we learned. She had only been four years old.

We transferred her out of Highland Terrace and she continued to excel marvelously. Of course, we talked to her that evening about the allegations. She cried. We cried. There were hugs. And for the first time in the four years she had lived with us, instead of Mama Saliki and Papa Saliki, she called us Mom and Dad. Our family was made flesh. Knit together in adversity.

How could it be otherwise?

III

We did our best by Our Girl. There are those, perhaps some of the very neighbors who open-arm welcomed us with casseroles and plates heaped high with homemade brownies, who now tut-tut and give quotes to reporters skulking behind our rosebushes and... but let us take you to the beginning of the end.

It started when they took the Whirlpool. Burly men in overalls daintily rang our doorbell, asked permission to come in please like they were popping over for afternoon tea – something innocuous and neighborly like Earl Grey. The ones who took the car were far less courteous; they disappeared it in the night-time while we lay fitfully in our beds, dreaming of bills come due and canceled credit cards.

We were having a few financial woes.

Doing our best in the face of career setbacks. Who knew an R&D chemist for General Mills could be downsized after twenty-two years? People were still eating their Wheaties. Someone was always after those Lucky Charms. And the demand for artfully arranged flowers had never been particularly high in our corner of this nominally Garden State. So things were tight, yet we were hopeful. We weren't keeping up with the Joneses. But we were keeping our obligations. People think Bono and Bill Gates are supporting the continent; they don't know it's us. Families like ours sending millions in remittances so cousin Manfred can have that corrective eye operation or paying the school fees for little Arabella in the village. That was us.

You have to understand how preoccupied we were back then. How desperate. Our Girl was seventeen years old, about to go off to a college whose tuition we could no longer afford. So we were slightly relieved when she said she wanted to put off school and live life for a bit. We were proud of this young woman. (When had she become such a woman, all hips and height?) She was better even than we had raised her to be, helping out around the house on weekends after we had to let the maid go. When had she learned about rinse cycles and pre-soaks or how to use all those special vacuum attachments? We had never even made her make her own bed.

She got a job. And two weeks later gave us an envelope thick with cash, just a little something to help out around the house. We didn't know where the money came from. We didn't want to know where the money came from. She was smart, she was enterprising, she was Our Girl.

This went on for months. Two weeks ago, Aunty Gladys was arrested. There are allegations of human trafficking and slavery and forced labor. A special prosecutor. Horrific testimonies from children she had placed with Cameroonian families all over the United States. One girl in Houston was forced to sleep on a pallet in the family's garage from the age of eight, tasked with cooking all the meals and caring for their three kids and cleaning the house. Another boy in Chicago was being sexually abused by the man of the house. Allegedly, Aunty Gladys would go to illiterate villagers and have them sign ad-hoc employment contracts, filling their heads with promises of educational advancement and money to support them. The courts contend that none of the children were sent to school. That they were little more than indentured servants, at their employers' beck and call day in and day out. The nominal pay they received (a pittance really at $30/week) was funneled back to their parents only after Aunty Gladys received her 50-per-cent processing fee. It was all coming to light.

Another light flashes beyond the gilded confines of our home.

We have been closeted here since the scandal broke. Blackout curtains drawn tight against the flash of camera bulbs.

The article on our family was in the *Post* today.

We are Page Six fodder, an exposé chockfull of doggerel and grainy, long-lens shots.

In the paper there are pictures of the 'house that whoring built', our rather unflattering driver's-license photos, and screen captures from Our Girl's website, Comely Cleaners, where she offers maid services – topless, they gleefully report. A service allegedly offered to half the neighborhood, at a discounted 'friends and family' rate, no less.

She had the decency to call us last night. To warn us.

'Why would you say those things, honey?' we cried. Broken.

'Because I needed to,' she said simply, her voice dry and crisp as fresh bills.

'But we love y… haven't we always been good to you? Given you everything you wanted?'

'Yes. You took me from my loving family so you could make my life better, right?' she said. 'You bought the best and taught me to want the best. To need and breathe it like air. You should be thrilled; the money they gave me for the story will pay for college and then some. Maybe I can parlay this into a book. Maybe a movie. Wish me well.'

She hung up then and we clung to each other. Shivering in the waning hours of the evening. We withdrew to our bedroom. On the nightstand in the master suite we found a creamy linen envelope. Inside: a diamond clasp with an eagle insignia; a ruby-studded tie-clip, and a note in Our Girl's meticulous handwriting that read simply:

To Mom and Dad,

For your troubles.

Your perfect daughter,

Winsome

Volume II: Their Girl

I

I give good read. Mais je suis rien commes des autres. Nothing like them. Those poor, poor telethon kids you scribble letters to and force-feed poto-poto rice 'for just ten cents a day'. Fly-haloed. Swollen tum-tums begging for your pre-tax dollars. You give and give and give again. #SaveOurKids. #BecauseYouCare. No, I am nothing like them, but I made your heartstrings twang with tabloid tales of my liberation from the Salikis, who took me when I was just a small nyango and made me Their Girl.

I was thirteen years old when she came for me; Mrs Fontep aka Ngando aka Dukong. First choice had been my follow-back, Arabella. Last cocoa in our family – age eight but could pass for the type of cuddly five-year-old you and your madame know from commercials where Happy Children™ eat Cheerios™ and Lucky Charms™ and everything is shine-shine. Bella was très mignon – a doll-baby with long, Hausa hair and a sweet-as-bonbon manner so unlike me, my maman's 'wahala pickin'.

'Perfect, perfect,' said Mrs Dukong.

At the center of our front parlor, Bella was twirling slowly for inspection in a dress Maman had fashioned from the remnants of an old okrika dress, its tattered lace made fine again by her hand. Maman just sat there next to Mrs Dukong, quiet as a mouet-mouet, head hanging low as over-ripe paw-paw. I was setting the table for our guest's meal. My ever-watchful grande soeur Frieda monitored from the kitchen doorway – neither in nor out.

'Does she speak proper English?' asked Mrs Dukong.

Do we speak proper English? Swine-beef! I wanted to tell that fatty bobolo, 'Nous sommes bilingues.' My family had lived in Douala for ten years now since Maman had come to make market – so we spoke 'proper' English and 'proper' French and pidgin and Franglais. Not like Mrs Dukong, with her pili-pili bush pronunciation grinding up 'proper' into 'pro-paah'.

I looked to Frieda, who looked at me and shook her head 'no.' So I folded my arms and sucked my teeth.

Mrs Dukong gave me some kind of eye.

'Do you have something to say, Zo... what is this one's name again?' she turned and asked Maman, who, without lifting her gaze from the ground, said: 'Don't mind her, Madame. That one is always talking.'

'I only wanted to say that the food is ready, Tantine.' I capped the lie with my best imitation Bella curtsey.

'No, no,' Mrs Dukong replied. 'I no get time for chop.'

At this, Maman finally lifted her head. We all stared. For weeks she had been preparing. Chey! Frieda have you dry-cleaned this floor? See me this girl. You want Madame to think we have no manners? Wahala pickin carry that new serving dish and go tchuk am high for shelf where Arabella cannot reach. She had been bartering her skills for weeks to make this dinner perfect. To buy gari that was a fine gold dust. Miraculously weevil-free sef-sef! For goat meat to put in the egusi stew, the butcher's wife received three new attires gratuit. Hmph. What made her too good for the bongo fish we usually ate it with? And why did we have to make show-show for people who were begging us for a child? People who were thiefing my sister.

'You'll not sit and eat, small-small?' Maman asked. 'I made the food special, secret family ingredients.'

'No, no. I cannot,' Mrs Dukong repeated.

Maman frowned.

We smiled.

Savoring the thought.

Our bellies biting.

'Very well. Well, well, Madeline,' Mrs Dukong finally said, sighing. 'I can see you went to some trouble. Pack the food. I will taste it and give the rest to my night-watch.'

She smiled at her generosity.

I was vexed sootay. This woman with all her juro-juro chins wobbling. Had she ever missed a meal in her whole life? Making me a langa dog sniffing for scraps in my own home!

I took the plate to the kitchen as instructed but scraped half into a bowl for my sisters and me to eat behind the house. The rest I put in maman's best new dish. Mixed in some tap water to puff it up again. Placed it on the floor between my legs, squatting to add in some of my own secret family ingredient. Hehehe.

I was humming when I returned to the parlor to find Mrs Dukong shouting. I thought of her 'special' soup and squared my shoulders, ready to deny or to fight. But I saw Arabella hiding behind Mama's skirt, crying until catarrh was coming from her nose.

'You tried to give me an Eboah!' said Mrs Dukong.

Oh. I forgot to mention that perfect Bella had a slight defect – a tiny limp, no worse than any other kids we knew in the quartier – with their bend-bend legs and rocking-pony gaits – all thanks to poorly dosed polio vaccinations at the free government clinic. Mrs Dukong yelled some more but Maman, who knew how to make market if she knew anything at all, began her best buyam-sellam spiel. She pulled me forward. Sold Mrs Dukong on how strong and hardworking I was.

'I don't need a housegirl–'

'She's top of her class–'

Yeah. I had been. Before I was kicked out of school for lack of school fees.

'She looks a bit old…'

'She's only ten, Madame.'

Mrs Dukong lifted an eyebrow.

'Sorry, I meant eleven, her birthday just passed.'

'Hmph. She will do.'

A month later I was shivering by a fireplace that looked like it could roast me whole like a goat. I was tired. I was hungry. And a little angry. I was what the Salikis wanted. And maybe a bit more than they bargained for.

Wasn't I worth it?

II

'How now, petite soeur? How you d–?'

My sister Frieda's face was stuck mid-question – all googly-eyed, hanging mop showing her gap-teeth. Hehehe. Our shaky Skype vid connection kept sputtering like a clando taxi at the motor-park. We had been talking for an hour and usually got cut off by now because Frieda always forgot to top off her phone minutes. In the hush,

I heard the Mother coming. Or rather the swish of the high blonde ponytail which forever swung behind her, agitating the air. She was in the open door to my bedroom, the one I wasn't allowed to lock until I officially turned sixteen. Two years from now by the Salikis' count. Two years ago by mine.

'Oh, nooo. The screen froze again?' she said. 'Do they need another cellphone?'

'It's fine, Madame,' said Frieda. Unfrozen. The Salikis had sent my family an iPhone with all types of social-media apps pre-loaded so we could keep in touch.

'Please, call me Jessica,' the Mother said.

'Thank you, Madame Jessica,' my sister replied. Frieda would never call her by her given name. Back home, we respected our elders. No matter how silly they were. Besides, Frieda didn't believe half the things I told her about the Mother because real parents never teetered on your Bieber bedspread to practice putting on lip-gloss with you, or asked you about your period and your feelings, or sashayed around in your Rock and Republic jeans humming because they've still 'got it'. Never. Ever.

Just a day ago, the Mother was blasting Kamer hip-hop, telling me, 'This new Jovi track na die!'

Seriously?

Frieda doesn't understand. The Salikis had plenty. In the beginning, they would always be hovering around me. Showing me their fine-fine clothing and their fine-fine jewelry like I had never seen such things. Like I was from the bush! The Mother always swishing her hair in my face like I couldn't buy my own horse-tail at the mall! But Frieda would look at screencaps of my perfect pink bedroom and curse me fine-fine for complaining. Tell me if I had stayed in Cameroon, I would have ended up like Maman with three kids, three different fathers, none of them her husband.

Frieda doesn't understand. It's a grind. Na hard work being one of the Happy Children™. Constant extra-currics: ballet on Tuesdays, riding lessons on Thursdays, daily violin, and an English tutor to help me speak better 'American'. Then there's school palava. The run-hide-fight active shooter drills in halls full of strapping blond boys who'd sooner bang-bang shoot you down than date you, it seemed. Their love on reserve for roving packs of perky girls: Amber (all twelve of her), Tiffani/y (the two with a 'y' and six with 'i' that she is), all looking right through you till you got the perfect Gucci knockoff and hair extensions like Kims K through Z. Everything fake. But at least, at least, some things come naturally. I was great at math, excuse me, mathematics, or, more accurately, AP algebra came easy. Like my maman, I had a head for figures.

Soon as they knew, the Salikis signed me up for Future Entrepreneurs Club. And Mathletics for good measure.

My sister and Madame Jessica chatted for a few

more minutes. Mainly Frieda's 'thank you, thank yous' for the new clothes sent to her and the rest of my 'six' siblings. Mrs Dukong was masterful at supplying official-looking documents from various boarding schools, at extracting ever-mounting school fees. Unlike me, Frieda had problems lying about make-believe kin. She made show-and-tell for the Mother, gathering Arabella and some small yam-heads from the quartier together for Skype sessions. Called me a lie-lie pickin. Though it didn't keep her from selling all that extra clothing to help fill Maman's new stall in the market – a side business selling American goods. Maman got a mean mark-up. We got something just for us. But sometimes Frieda's boyfriend Boniface helped manage the store when Maman was busy sewing. I didn't trust him with a register full of our hard-earned nkap. And I didn't bite my tongue about saying so. Ey-ey! The yam-head was a cut-purse – okay, okay – that's 'pickpocket' in American. Former cut-purse, Frieda said. Then she said I was a hypocrite. My hands were way down deep in the Salikis' pockets, no be so?

'Not hypocritical, grande soeur,' I said. 'Entrepreneurial. That's me.'

Wasn't I worth it?

II

I did what I had to. For myself. For my family's future. Mrs Dukong discovered Maman's kiosk and demanded her cut. Grubby hands in every pot. And the well was running dry. The Salikis were struggling. So I got entrepreneurial.

It began with heartbreak. One of those strapping blond boys finally took a liking. Imagine! An American boyfriend of my very own! But for months his gaze kited over me in school corridors. I went dateless at three dances. After a time, it dawned on me. I was too dark for daylight hours. I was low, felt invisible. But I yam what I yam, so I rallied. And soon another came along – big, brawny – his people hailing from somewhere along the country's midriff. I looked at him and saw plenty: fattened calves, amber waves of grain. He looked at me and saw exotica: spears, breasts – everything jutting. He would fuck me for novelty, then marry his corn-fed sweetie. But this time round I would get something. Treasured. A keepsake. My own little piece of America.

My trinkets attracted corn-fed girls. They go gaga for show-show bling, for bedazzled cellies and pink-sequined UGGs. They want so much more than Daddy's Little Girl deserves. So I taught them how to find new daddies, ones seeking sugar babies. It worked so well I set up a site. And soon another, for maid services au naturel. It was easy. This is a land where homemade XXX equals endorsements, a rapper hubby and an iPhone app of your very own. Sex always, always sells.

Question was: how to keep Mrs Dukong out of

my profit margins?

So I gathered intel, touched base with some of the other children she had airdropped in barely vetted homes across the US.

A girl in Houston. Sleeping on pallet? No!

Another boy in Chicago. They touched you down there? You don't say?

Horrific tales, all.

My mission? Accomplished. Had all the ammunition needed and then some.

Don't judge. It was war. Kill or be killed.

So by the time they took the Whirlpool I was ready. A sugar-daddy client knew a guy who knew a guy who worked at the *Post*. A week later, Aunty Gladys was arrested. There were allegations of human trafficking and slavery and forced labor. A special prosecutor appointed.

My interview is in the *Post* today. My side hustles too salacious to pass up in print. It was publicity for my businesses – Comely Cleaners set to double its customer base.

It really was never meant to be about the Salikis. My story is my own to tell.

Said as much when I called them last night.

Listening as they blubbered about all the things they'd done for me.

For me? Seriously? It was me who made them a family. I'm the one that made them real. 'Wasn't I worth it?' I asked. 'I was snatched up from my loving family so yours could be complete. All this talk of giving me the American Dream. Then, just like that, you're raiding my college fund.'

'We had a mortgage to pay!' they cried. 'You needed a roof over your head!'

'I needed a future,' I said finally. 'And now I've made sure I'll have one.'

I hung up. Left them to their tears and seltzer water.

Tucked away in my hotel bed, I dreamed of better. Maybe I could parlay my story into a book. Or a Lifetime movie at the very least. I pictured the opening credits.

Based upon a true story. With my true name in bright lights...

Zora.

Ngwah-Mbo Nana Nkweti is a Cameroonian-American writer and graduate of the Iowa Writers' Workshop. She is the recipient of fellowships and residencies from MacDowell, Vermont Studio Center, Ucross, Byrdcliffe, Kimbilio, Virginia Center for the Creative Arts, Clarion West, Hub City, the Wurlitzer Foundation and the Stadler Center for Poetry and Literary Arts. Nana's writing has been published in journals and magazines such as *Brittle Paper, New Orleans Review* and *The Baffler*, amongst others. Her forthcoming short-story collection, *Like Walking on Cowry Shells*, focuses on the lives of hyphenated-Americans who share her multicultural heritage in the United States and Africa. 'It Takes A Village Some Say' was first published in *The Baffler*.

All Our Lives

Tochukwu Emmanuel Okafor

We are city people. We live in wooden shacks alongside lagoons that smell of decaying fish and shit. We live in rented apartments with flush toilets and airy bedrooms. We live under bridges, with torn tarpaulins to cover us, feet pounding and vehicles speeding above our heads. The air in this city is rancid with sweat, gas flares, and sun-warmed garbage. Some of us live in face-me-I-face-yous. We are tired of the daily bickering with our neighbours. Of the lack of privacy. Of infections contracted from pit latrines. We wish we had our own homes. Homes full of servants and pets, with pretty gardens, and fences to shield us from the foulness of this city.

We are Chikamneleanya, Ogheneakporobo, Abdulrasheed, Olarenwaju, Alamieyeseigha, Tamu-nodiepriye, Onuekwuchema, Toritsemugbone, or Oritshetimeyin. We are twenty-five, twenty-six, twenty-seven years old. We are from the North, South, Southeast. Some of us do not know where we come from. We are tall, plump, lanky, short.

We speak Igbo, Yoruba, Kalabari, Hausa, Itshekiri, Ijaw, pidgin English, or a mix of them all. We are Catholics, Pentecostals, Muslims, Adventists. We do not believe in any god. We are single, we have wives and children that we have left behind in our villages. We come from families of five, eight, ten. Or we come from polygamous homes. Or we do not know if we have families at all. We like to eat akpu and ofe ogbonno, eba and gbegiri, amala, tuwo, beans, rice. We do not eat salad or chicken or pizza because they are expensive.

Each morning before leaving for our workplaces and each evening before bedtime, we gaze into the mirror and touch our faces, thinking of ourselves as ugly, pimply, handsome, beautiful. Our noses are like those of our ancestors – bulbous, pinched in the corners, fat, aquiline, straight, or scarred. We braid our hair into dreadlocks or in neat corn-rows, or we leave our hair to grow into Afros. We are bald. We crop our hair low, or our hair is unkempt, tufts of foam with lice nesting in them. We are black. We are not black. We bleach our skin. We refuse to bleach our skin since we toil under the sun – we do not want the heat to scald us, leaving patches of red here and streaks of black there.

We are newspaper vendors, taxi drivers, waiters, housekeepers. In this city where the buildings breathe into each other, and the power lines are thin black criss-crosses in the skies, we hustle, threading our paths in a busy crowd. We look for customers. Some days, when we make good sales, we are happy. We buy drinks. We invite our friends to join us. We eat salad, chicken, or pizza. We thank God in many languages. Other days, we endure insults from customers. We curse the day we were born. We do not thank God. We survive for long stretches without food. We fold our arms and watch the government take down trees to erect mega city halls. Yet we have no proper homes. We have no light. We have no water.

At four, five, six, we were running naked around the dusty grounds of our villages. We attended schools that had no blackboards or desks or libraries. We never went to school. The lucky ones among us were taken away to live with a rich uncle or an oga and madam, who turned us into slaves and made us sell wares on the street. We raced each other to see who was the fastest. We shot down birds with our catapults and planted traps for antelopes. Later, we presented the game to our mothers who praised us and then carried them into their kitchens, to cook meat soup. We sat around small fires, opening our mouths to chew the scents escaping our mothers' pots, hearing our bellies groan as we swallowed. We told one another stories. We were happy, comfortable. We were enough.

At fifteen, sixteen, seventeen, we were chasing girls. We attacked them at streams, or in dark corners where they gathered in fours and fives to gossip. We squeezed their breasts and ran away. They pursued us, hurling curses at our grandfathers and great-grandfathers. At home, we refused to wash the hands that had touched them. We smelled our palms and imagined things. By night, we played with our manhoods with those hands, shutting our eyes tight. Not once, not twice, our mothers caught us. They laughed and said: Obere nwoke. Keremin mutum. Small man. *You don't even know how to catch a woman.* But we knew we were champions. After all, there were other boys who shied away from girls, who had never come close enough to touch a breast. We were different. We were men. We knew how to hunt, farm, fight, kill, grab breasts. The girls enjoyed it, but they pretended not to. They strutted around the place, ululating praises to their gods as their feet slap-slapped past us, thanking them for the gift of sun, rain and future responsible husbands. We knew they would be ours one day, or not. Or we knew better, classier women awaited us in the depths beyond our villages.

At nineteen, twenty, twenty-one, this was how we dreamt. We found ourselves walking down an expanse of gold-carpeted road. On both sides of the road, trees climbed into the skies. They bore bananas, apples, mangoes, avocados, all the fruits we could imagine. As we walked down the road, animals – monkeys, goats, tortoise, rabbits, lions – bowed, waving at us after we had stepped further away. At the end of the road, a neem tree whistled, twisting towards us. Its branches swayed in the breeze, and it lowered itself before us, urging us to climb its trunk. We obeyed. We held on tight. The neem tree straightened and grew and grew. Eventually we climbed off onto the clouds. We shielded our eyes; it was bright all around. A gate creaked open. We saw people lying flat on their bellies, singing, *All Hail the King*. We marched on their bare backs and walked on into glass mansions that were ours and ours alone. House servants fell on their knees, welcoming us. We walked past great fleets of cars, past gardens square and verdant, past pools clearer than the skies, and on into enormous palaces. We sat on thrones. In this dream, we owned the city. We owned the people. We owned power.

At twenty, twenty-one, twenty-two, we were leaving our homes in the villages. Our mothers cried their hearts out. They said, *Who will bury us when we leave this world?*

Us, we answered.

Who will take care of us when we are old, guiding our paths when our eyes grow tired?

We kept silent.

Who will look after the wives and children you have left behind?

Silence.

Who will marry our girls?

No reply.

When will you return?

When we are rich and famous and own people and power, we said.

Fools, they called us. *You cannot even weed your fathers' farms properly. What makes you think you will make it in the city? The city is full of night women who will steal your senses. The city will devour you.*

Still, we packed our few clothes, wrapped them in raffia baskets, wide linen wrappers, polythene bags. We left. Our mothers cried. Our fathers gazed into the night.

We are now city people. We can be Matt, Jason, Alex, Garth, Arthur. We can be twenty, twenty-one, twenty-two. We can come from London, New York, Paris, or any other exotic place our fingers can never locate on a map. We can be tall, athletic, broad, sinewy, thick. Our hair is auburn, rooty blond, steel grey. We can speak American English, garnishing our sentences with 'wanna' and 'gonna'; flecks of 'fuck,' 'holy fuck,' 'shit,' 'damn' or 'nigger'. We act like we own stretches and stretches of land, stately homes, estates, penthouses. We say we are cousins to the President of the United States, grandsons of the Queen of England, close friends with the Prime Minister of France. We carry ourselves like people who don't shit.

This is the year the internet arrives in our city.

The cybercafés are our second homes. They are tight spaces on ground floors in one- or two-storey buildings. Because the government never provides us with regular power, you can hear generators, chained outside to metal rails to stave off thieving boys, bleating into the day and night. All night, mosquitoes sing into our ears, their songs louder than the clacks of our fingers on the keyboards. We rub insect repellent onto ourselves until our skin is waxen.

By night, the internet is so fast that the drowsiness in our eyes flees. We download photos from websites we cannot recall. A wiry-built white man baring his chest. An African-American, grinning, his hair tousled, both ears studded in a full semi-circle. Hunks. Perfect jaws. Perfect cheekbones. Glorious bodies. By night, we glow in these bodies that are not our own.

Do not think we are searching for love. Love does not exist in this city. We are men of the night. Our reward is money.

In the beginning, we fill in lengthy forms on dating sites. We keep a note of the sites we have signed up for: Matchmake.org CupidHearts.net DateMe.com. We begin with our sisters who live in the more comfortable African cities: Johannesburg, Cape Town, Douala, Windhoek, Accra. They are foolish, these sisters. See how they bare their breasts on screen, as though they are a thing for sale, raw meat displayed at a marketplace, flies and dust licking at them. *Whores*, we call them. *Darlings*, they call us.

Will you take us to America? they ask.

Yeah, baby, we say.

Do we get to fly first class?

Yeah, baby. And you're gonna roll in my jet and watch the world beneath you fade to nothing.

Darling, you are so sweet, you make me wet.

Yeah, baby. You are sweeter.

The sisters loyal to their families ask if they can bring along sick parents and younger siblings who have been sent off as apprentices. They ask if they can bring their favourite aunts and uncles. *Do they make masala chai in Texas? Can a decent meal of bobotie be bought in the streets of London? Baby, I hear there are tall tall buildings and many Rocky Mountains and the weather is always freezing cold in Canada, will there be gardens at least to plant ukazi?* We tell them, *Yes, yes, yes.*

It is upon their eagerness that we feed. But this eagerness dies all too quickly when we ask them to send money.

Darling, they say, *you are rich. What do you need my money for?*

Baby, we begin, *issues with the bank. The fucking account is frozen.*

And this is how we watch them delete us from their lives. Sometimes, they ignore our online presence. Other times, they ask, *Baby, have you sorted out the problem with your bank account?* We do not reply. We pay heavily for the internet. Time is a luxury. We cannot waste it on them.

The city is a fat, dark aunt with a tight-lipped smile, who embraces her prodigal sons. Yet, she cares little for them. She churns and churns us until we are millet chaff that the strong breeze sloughs off. And we drift deeper and deeper into the pitch-dark corners of her home. We lose our jobs. We lose the shelters where we once lived. We roam the streets.

By day, we climb into molues – those rickety peeling buses, whose insides smell of all things foul and rotten, compressing us, sticks in a matchbox. We pick pockets. Sometimes, we are lucky. We swindle fine leather wallets and purses, and, in them, wads and wads of crisp notes. We celebrate festive seasons like everyone else in this city, with chickens and beer and cheap, russet-haired women we coax off the streets. Other times, we are unlucky. Some of us get caught, dragged off the molues, and beaten with clubs and machetes, until our bodies are bloodied canvasses. Some of us have our fingers chopped off. Some of us sleep in tight cells where older inmates sink cigarette ends into our bare backs. We scream and scream. The city does not hear us.

We return to the internet, to our second homes. Now we choose to be women online. Black women flaunting bodies with an oily sheen. We visit websites that we cannot recall, downloading photos of the women we are pretending to be. At first, we are shocked by what we have become – our sisters, who have cast aside the dignity of their bodies. Now we are them, parading our *assets*, toying with ourselves, laughing in our borrowed nakedness. Still, we glower. We wonder if there are still good girls we can marry and take home to our dream mansions. In our hearts, we are angry with our sisters for their cheapness. We hope they come back to themselves from this place in which they are lost. But who says we are not lost too?

In our stolen bodies, we create new profiles on new dating sites. The sites seem to multiply every day as though they are birthing children and grandchildren who can no longer recognize their ancestry. Each one struggles to outperform the other with its new features: voice chat, live cam, a 'viewed profile' check-box, location filtering, custom avatars. We meet men who are gullible enough to buy anything – a bra, a necklace, a handbag – if we tell them it has touched our skin.

Perverts, we call them. Old white men, with streaks of greying hair and lined skin. We detest them, but they promise us the whole of the States. First, they send postcards. We never look at them. Then they send pictures of their burly selves in thickly wooded hills. *Me going camping, hun*, the handwritten caption says. Then they send half-naked pictures of themselves, beer in hand, sitting on a patio. A patio we long to sit on, breathing in American air and watching cars and flimsily dressed skinny white women amble by, white wafers from the skies landing and melting down our parched throats. We tell these old men that we wish to come to the States, to Paris, to London. We beg them. We say we will be their slaves. We say we will let them have us any way they know how to. We say we are dying to bring their children into the world.

They send money. Chunks of foreign currencies. We rush to the banks, smiling. We convert the money into our local currency. We feast. We jam the city with loud music. We close off streets, invite the world to our celebrations and have the best of young women. Sometimes we remember home. We send money and gifts, imagining our mothers dancing around the villages, eulogizing us, our fathers gazing skyward, thanking their gods for the generous blessings. The foreigners ask if we have received the money. We don't answer. We shut down our accounts on the dating sites and set up new ones elsewhere.

Or.

Some of us are unlucky; they do not send money. They say they are going through a divorce and are heavily in debt. They curse their ex-wives. They tell us to get a loan from a bank or a family member. They promise to pay back the loan when we arrive in their foreign lands. When we tell them that we are incapable of obtaining loans, they rail at us. They threaten to stop loving us. Soon our chats dwindle, and we become strangers. We part ways.

We are tired of our fake lives. We are bored. We become ourselves again, or we become partly ourselves, or we give up on cyberlove for a while. We take pictures of slums and send them to foreign organizations, and foreign men and women to whom we profess our love. We beg for their pity. We say we are poor Africans who sniff glue, or poor Africans who exhume freshly buried people and roast their flesh for food, or poor Africans fleeing tribal wars.

Or we do not say we are poor Africans. We act like normal people who wish to love and be loved. We are humans, after all. Our own needs are valid, too. We send pictures that show us garbed in our Sunday best – in clothes that are tailored from kaftan, brocade, kente or akwa-oche. We long to marry our online dates, to be absorbed into another world so different from this city, but we cannot afford to cross the city's border. We do anything to get our lovers to send money. We take nude photos of ourselves. We film scenes of self-pleasuring. We record ourselves dancing naked. They get excited. They mail us tickets. We leave, or we do not leave.

Some of us encounter a different kind of love, and the city tries to lynch us. A cybercafé manager has caught us visiting sites where men seek love from their fellow men. Men kissing men, one sucking the other's manhood, each taking turns to ply themselves from behind. At first, we are disgusted. Our minds scream abomination. We wonder how a man can find joy in another man's body. How unnatural it is that the love between them is consummated through the small hole where shit exits the body. We don't understand this kind of love. We are confused when our bodies begin to respond to such passions, longing to be explored by men. We imagine men's lips crushing against ours. We imagine being held at night. We yearn for this different kind of love.

But the city is spitting us out. It has had enough of us. The police want to take us off to cells that smell of shit and never see daylight. The people are burning our homes and demanding our heads. We are fleeing. We are placeless. The city no longer recognizes us. The skies burst open, drenching the littleness that is left of us. We leave our dreams behind. We cross the city's border. We take up new lives.

Tochukwu Emmanuel Okafor is a Nigerian writer whose work has appeared in the 2018 *Best of the Net*, the 2019 *Best Small Fictions*, *The Guardian*, Harvard's *Transition Magazine*, *Columbia Journal*, and elsewhere. A 2018 Rhodes Scholar finalist and a 2018 Kathy Fish Fellow, he has won the 2017 Short Story Day Africa Prize for Short Fiction. He has been shortlisted for the 2018 *Brittle Paper* Award for Fiction, the 2017 Awele Creative Trust Award, the 2016 Problem House Press Short Story Prize, and the 2016 *Southern Pacific Review* Short Story Prize. He lives in Pittsburgh, USA, and is at work on a novel and a short-story collection. 'All Our Lives' was first published in *ID Identity: New Short Fiction From Africa* (Short Story Day Africa/New Internationalist 2018).

Support literary and cultural excellence from Africa through the Caine Prize for African Writing

"Over the years, the Caine Prize has done a great deal to foster writing in Africa and bring exciting new African writers to the attention of wider audiences"

J.M. Coetzee, Nobel Prize Laureate for Literature

About Us

The Caine Prize for African Writing was launched in 2000 with the aim of encouraging and highlighting the rich diversity of African writing by bringing it to a wider, international audience. The prize is named after the late Sir Michael Caine, Chairman of the 'Africa 95' arts festival in Europe and Africa in 1995 and for nearly 25 years Chairman of the Booker Prize management committee. We are a registered charity whose aim is to bring African writing to a wider audience using our annual literary award. We do not benefit from an endowment and rely on raising funds to continue our work each year. We are passionate and committed to seeing Africa's stories told in all their nuance and complexity and welcome your support of our mission.

HOW TO GIVE

To find out more about how to give please visit:
www.caineprize.com/donate

If you would like to enquire about sponsorship and partnership with the Caine Prize, please email:
info@caineprize.com

The Caine Prize rules of entry

The Caine Prize is awarded annually to a short story by an African writer published in English, whether in Africa or elsewhere. The prize has become a benchmark for excellence in African writing.

An 'African writer' is taken to mean someone who was born in Africa, or who is a national of an African country, or who has a parent who is African by birth or nationality.

The indicative length is between 3,000 and 10,000 words.

There is a cash prize of £10,000 for the winning author, £500 for each shortlisted writer and a travel award for each of the shortlisted candidates (up to five in all).

For practical reasons, unpublished work and work in other languages is not eligible. Works translated into English from other languages are not excluded, provided they have been published in translation and, should such a work win, a proportion of the prize would be awarded to the translator.

The award is made in July each year, the deadline for submissions being 31 January. The shortlist is selected from work published in the five years preceding the submissions deadline and not previously considered for a Caine Prize. Submissions, including those from online journals, should be made by publishers and will need to be accompanied by six original published copies of the work for consideration, sent to the address below. There is no application form.

Every effort is made to publicize the work of the shortlisted authors through broadcast, online and printed media.

Winning and shortlisted authors will be invited to participate in writers' workshops in Africa and elsewhere as resources permit.

The above rules may be modified in the light of experience.

The Caine Prize
Menier Chocolate Factory
51 Southwark Street
London, SE1 1RU, UK
Telephone: +44 (0)20 7378 6234
Email: info@caineprize.com
Website: caineprize.com
Find us on Facebook, Twitter @caineprize and Instagram.